Ropebait

Hal Bannion's Broken Spur ranch is in deep trouble. During a drunken spree Hal's brother John, having broken all his promises, has gambled away the ranch to the Bannions' arch enemy, Charles Ashby.

Now, returning weary from the dangers of the trail, Hal suspects dirty dealing and sets out to win back the Broken Spur. Fortunately, he is not alone as, years before, Hal's late father saved Miguel Santos' son from a lynch mob and Santos is determined to repay the debt.

Can he escape a hangman's noose, dodge hot lead and assert his rightful claim to his ranch without ending up on Boot Hill?

ROPEBAIT

SKEETER DODDS

A Black Horse Western

ROBERT HALE · LONDON

© Skeeter Dodds 2001
First published in Great Britain 2001

ISBN 0 7090 6861 1

Robert Hale Limited
Clerkenwell House
Clerkenwell Green
London EC1R 0HT

Typeset by
Derek Doyle & Associates, Liverpool.
Printed and bound in Great Britain by
Antony Rowe Limited, Wiltshire

ONE

The single bullet that whipped Hal Bannion's Stetson into the air and flapped his longish auburn hair, screwed off a boulder behind him, buzzed like an angry bee around the small horse-shoe canyon into which he had driven the horses, and whined away to die in an unidentified place.

Hal didn't move a muscle. He resisted the urge to dive into the tumble of nearby boulders for cover; cover he'd never make. Whoever the shooter was could have as easily split his skull open as lifting the Stetson from his head. His shot had been inch perfect. It was not a lucky shot; the shooter handled a rifle with the skill of an ace marksman.

The Bannion crew also recognized a marksman when they saw one in action and, like Hal, knew that their name was on a bullet if they budged.

'Stay right where you are, boys,' Hal ordered,

hoping fear wouldn't override their good sense. 'Scatter, and I doubt if any one of you will make it to cover.'

'What'll we do, Hal?' Ben Rogers, Hal's right hand man asked in a hoarse whisper. 'Sit pretty?'

'That's about all we can do,' Hal replied, 'until whoever's got us in his sights makes his business known.'

It could only have been seconds before the Mexican bandit appeared on the rim of the canyon, but it seemed like an eternity.

'Hey, *amigos*,' he called in a friendly voice that fooled no one, 'you got nice horses that Pancho Morientes, that's me, *señors*, theenks you should share with your friends.'

Hal called back, 'Share?'

'Yes, Señor Bannion.'

'He's done his homework, I'll give him that,' Hal Bannion sighed.

'Half for you, half for me, eh, *amigo*?' Morientes laughed with the ease of a man holding a winning hand. His drooping belly quivered with mirth. 'Good deal, Yanqui, yes?'

'You ain't going to hand over half to that greasepot, are yah, Hal?' Ben Rogers enquired.

Hal reminded Rogers, 'We don't exactly hold the upper hand, Ben.'

'You think that pox-ridden bastard will settle for half anyway? With us over a barrel?'

'Nope. But we've got to play for time!'

Rogers growled. 'Sounds to me like you're ready to deal, Hal.'

Hal, annoyed by Rogers' criticism answered curtly. 'Horses ain't any good to a dead man.'

'Señor Bannion,' the bandit leader called. He waved his arm and a small army of greasy cut-throats appeared in the canyon boulders and on the rim. 'Under the circumstances, my offer is a generous one. I peeck, *amigo*.'

'We just can't let that whore's spit take half, Hal,' Rogers argued.

'I damn well ain't goin' to stand for being ripped off nohow,' a small bow-legged man, name of Jack Brandy, spat. He flung his plate of beans aside and sprang to his feet. A rifle cracked and Brandy's head exploded, spattering the other men with blood and fragments of bone.

'Hey, *amigos*,' Morientes called again, as the canyon rattled to the readying of rifles, 'do not be fooleesh.'

Bannion, resigned to losing half, if not all of the horses that were intended to save him and his brother from destitution, agreed. 'We can do business, Morientes.'

'Sensible decision, Yanqui!'

'There's not a thing we can do,' Hal said to the grim-faced men. 'There's at least twenty rifles on us, and we've already got one widow!'

The bandit leader waved his arm and more men came out of the depths of the canyon, rifles trained on Hal Bannion and his partners. They spread out to encircle them, before Morientes changed his terms.

'You know, Yanquis, I forget to tell you that Pancho Morientes is a greedy man. I theenk I want all of your horses, my friends.'

More bandits appeared from different parts of the canyon to begin rounding up the horses. However, the miracle that Hal had been praying for came to pass. Suddenly the men flanking Morientes on the rim of the canyon, fell in a hail of lead, tumbling down into the canyon, bouncing from boulder to boulder like rag dolls, ending on the canyon floor crushed and bloodied. The suddenness of the intervention, by as yet unseen forces, handed Hal and his men the gift of surprise and more than half the circle of bandits around them dropped under their spitting guns.

Morientes scrambled over the rim of the canyon and went in a running crouch to scramble down the sliding shale path, until he lost control of the treacherous conditions underfoot and crashed headlong into a jagged boulder that ripped open his chest on impact.

The remaining bandits stumbled around like headless chickens, to be picked off by a line of Mexicans led by Miguel Santos, who took up position on the rim of the canyon. Excited by the scent of blood and the thunder of guns the horses stampeded. As they charged out of the canyon, those bandits in their tracks were mangled under the horses' angry hooves. It took a long time for their screams to sink into the walls of the canyon.

'Don't worry my friend,' Miguel Santos called, as Hal watched despairingly at the vanishing horses. 'My men will round them up.'

Hal went to meet the Mexican, whose horses the bandits had tried to steal, and embraced him in gratitude.

'One of my men brought word that Pancho Morientes and his cut-throats were raiding peasant villages along the Rio Grande. I knew that such fine horses would prove too much of a temptation for him.'

'How can I ever repay you, Miguel?' Hal asked.

Miguel Santos put his arm around the shoulders of a young man standing at his side, and said, 'Your father gave me back my son, that is my reward, Hal Bannion. I will give you an escort across the Rio Grande to make sure that none of Morientes' friends will covet your goods. God go with you, my friend.'

'And with you, Miguel.'

'*Adios!*'

The next morning, an hour after sun-up, Hal Bannion crossed the Rio Grande, believing that his dream of saving the ranch he had struggled to keep going, and would have certainly lost except for Miguel Santos' extraordinary generosity in repaying a debt he owed Hal's late father, Tom, would come true.

Tom Bannion had saved Pedro Santos, Miguel's only son, from the clutches of a brood of vipers six years before, when Pedro had come to visit a girl on the side of the Rio where the red-neck trio who'd set upon him, reckoned a Mex shouldn't be.

They had a rope around his neck when Tom Bannion happened along. Miguel Santos promised that day that if ever he could, he would repay his debt to Hal's father. The chance never came when Tom Bannion was alive, but Miguel Santos had honoured his pledge to Hal, and just in time. Another couple of months, at most, and the Broken Spur, Tom Bannion's life's work, would have been lost to the bank first, and then to Charles Ashby.

And if that ever happened, Tom Bannion would spin in his grave.

TWO

Hal Bannion looked with pride on the moon-washed horses he'd driven back across the Rio Grande; healthy horses that would be readily purchased by the army.

'I ain't rightly sure about this plan of yours, Hal.'

John Bannion's words came back to Hal and, though he could afford to smile like a well-fed cat now, he, too, had had his doubts when he'd set out two weeks before with every cent they had to buy the horses from Miguel Santos for a fraction of their true worth.

'The horses are yours for nothing, my friend,' Santos had generously offered.

Hal had his pride, which was already badly dented by his beggar's quest. 'I'll pay what I can, Señor Santos. And when the horses are sold, I will pay the rest.'

'There is no need,' Santos had assured him. 'How can a man put a price on his only son's life, or on your father's misery? What is the gift of a few horses compared to your father's sacrifice, *señor*?'

For his neighbourly intervention in Pedro Santos' lynching, Tom Bannion, a week later, had earned a bullet in the back from a bushwhacker's gun, that left him with a shattered spine and useless legs. Helplessly, Hal and John Bannion had watched their father's pride shrivel, and despair take over until he went early to his Maker to join his wife who had fallen to an Indian arrow years before, in the days when Indian trouble was a fact of life.

His beloved Sarah gone, Tom Bannion had toiled from sun-up to sunset to make the Broken Spur one of the finest ranches in Texas. The Spur wasn't big, Texas style, but every inch of it was good steer fattening grass. Tom had hewn a channel from solid rock to trap a sparkling mountain stream the water of which kept the range protected from the dry winds that could turn grass to brittle straw and moist soil to sand. The Broken Spur was the envy of bigger spreads and had, over the years, earned the attention of greedy eyes.

At the time their father had been backshot, Hal and John Bannion had not yet reached manhood and weren't much use around the place except to perform chores. Soon the Broken Spur was in trouble, and had gone steadily downhill. When Tom Bannion had died a broken man, and from the moment his coffin was covered, the vultures began to gather. Finally, despite Hal and John's best efforts, the bank had called in the brothers and given them the bad news about their finances.

'Foreclosure, ain't fair!' Hal had protested.

'And there'll be no need to foreclose,' Andrew Barrett, the bank president, emphasized, 'if you boys will accept Mr Ashby's generous offer to purchase the Broken Spur.'

'Over my dead body!' Hal had spat.

'Then the bank has no choice,' Barrett had told them. 'I need payment of your debt, or . . .' Barrett's predatory mood had then softened. 'Hal, John, I knew and loved your father. He was a fine and good man, and if I could turn a blind eye I would. But the bank has shareholders who expect a healthy return on their investment.'

'Shareholders like Charles Ashby!'

'Among others.' Barrett shook his head. 'You boys are being stubborn and foolish. Ashby will get his hands on the Broken Spur anyway, once the bank forecloses, and for half the price he'll have to pay you. Accept his offer, boys.'

'Never!' Hal and John Bannion had said in unison, both men recalling Ashby's sneers every time he set eyes on their crippled father. It was

Ashby's hardcases' idea of fun that the Broken Spur boss had thwarted when he saved Pedro Santos' neck from a noose. The general opinion was that Tom Bannion had not made his wisest move in bucking Ashby or his henchmen, and it wasn't the first time. Most folk figured that the bushwhacker's bullet that grounded the Broken Spur rancher was Charles Ashby's pay-back.

'Then I see no hope,' Andrew Barrett had said. 'I can give you a month or two, I guess. But that's all.'

Hearing of the Bannions' plight, Miguel Santos sent word to Hal that he would give him the horses free, and await payment until Hal had sold the horses to the army. It would not be charity; it would be hard work deserving of reward. The army would buy all the horses of sound wind that they could get their hands on, and pay well for them.

Now Hal's own words that he used to quell his brother John's doubts came back to him.

'It's a gamble, John. The thing is, if we just sit, we're finished for sure.'

'You bring back the finest hooves you can, Hal,' John had murmured on the starlit porch the night before Hal had left. 'I'll wait right here and get things ready.'

John Bannion had always been more a carpenter than a rancher, loving the things he could do with wood. The kitchen dresser, made of sturdy but beautiful mountain oak, was a delight to behold and had admirers coming from miles around to view it.

He'd promised, 'As sure as God's my judge, I won't sup a single drop, Hal.'

In recent times, imbibing had become more than a leisurely pastime for John Bannion.

Hal fashioned a smoke and settled down to puff, pondering as men had from the beginning of time about the star-filled sky and the glory of its Creator. The six men he'd hired to make the trip to Mexico with him were long since asleep, but Bannion didn't mind; he'd always liked the still of night. That's when he did most of his dreaming, and he'd been dreaming about horse ranching for quite a spell now; in fact, since he was nine years old and his father had come home drawing a piebald pony behind the supply wagon for which he'd traded beef with an Indian. It was that very day that Hal promised himself that one day he'd have a range chockful of fine, high-stepping horses, and that dream was about to become a reality.

'Almost home, John,' he sighed.

He rolled into his blanket, jiggling about on the stony ground until he found a spot that was half comfortable. He'd sleep with one eye open, as he'd done since leaving the Santos ranch. He was in dangerous country, full of predators, so the vigil to stay alive was a constant one. They'd been lucky so far. The Mex bandit, Morientes, had paid a

heavy price, but if Miguel Santos had not intervened, it would have been his and his crew's bones
bleaching. They had crossed the Rio Grande, and
could not count on Santos' intervention should
trouble come again. There were still plenty of
Americanos who would be more than eager to
avoid the work but enjoy the profits. And there
was the threat of drifting Indians who had left the
reservations.

Hal Bannion needed more men than he had,
but he had all he could afford, and they, with the
exception of Ben Rogers a long-time friend and
ally, would probably hightail it than risk their
hides again, for the wages that Hal could afford to
pay, with a down-the-line-promise of more when
he sold the horses. He'd not expect any man to
risk his life for his dream, and there were one or
two who might very well throw in with any
thieves who made the right offer. Hal reckoned his
biggest risk now came from rawhiders; the kind of
scum that valued a man to the penny; human
vultures whose nature was even meaner.

Bannion said a quiet prayer that his luck would
hold. If it did, tomorrow night the horses would be
nestling in the corrals that John would have
ready. From there, the Broken Spur would be on
the road to better days; the kind of happy days
that it had enjoyed under the care of a strong and
healthy Tom Bannion, when the Spur was the
kind of ranch that men both admired and envied

for its success. Hal's father had been generous in sharing his secrets with men who now watched and waited as the Broken Spur ailed, hoping to grab its rich valley grass and rock-cool water for pennies when the bank foreclosed.

'But they'll damn well not be getting their greedy paws on one blade of Broken Spur grass, or a mouthful of its clean water,' Hal vowed. 'And especially that hog, Charles Ashby!'

The venomous surge of hate that accompanied mention of Ashby's name left no doubt about Hal Bannion's feelings for the saloon owner at Crosby Flats, the town that serviced the ranches and farms that worked the fertile lands of the plains and valleys to the south of the town, before the earth turned to grit and powder and became useless as it ran into the desert country beyond. It was a constant battle to stop the encroaching desert. Hal, like his father before him, fought an on-going battle to maintain the soil's rich fertility by diverting water through a network of ducts to keep the desert at bay. It was a constant war that the ranchers and farmers had to fight against nature, and usually it was a shared and neigh-bourly one, but since Tom Bannion's death, it had been a lonely fight for the Broken Spur.

John Bannion had made a nuisance of himself more than once while in his cups, upsetting Luther Bramwell, the most influential *hombre* in this neck of the woods, and folk had become downright unneighbourly towards the Bannions and outright unheeding of the Broken Spur's crisis.

'Everyone kicks a dog when he's down, Hal,' Andrew Barret had wisely predicted early on in the Broken Spur's slide. 'There'll be some hoping to pick up a bargain, and there'll be others content to take pleasure in your misfortune. Your father was a proud, independent and sometimes abrasive man. That is a legacy which, as a Bannion, passes to you.'

It troubled Hal that his brother had developed a fondness for liquor. Being fragile of mind, the hopelessness since their father's passing had worked on John's nerves. Not being of a ranching frame of mind, Hal had urged his brother to seek his fortune in carpentry. Settlers arrived all the time, towns grew and new ones sprang up. Crosby Flats and the surrounding countryside alone would keep John busily and gainfully employed. He had often talked about his dream of opening a furniture store, predicting, much to most folks' amusement, that one day towns like Crosby Flats would have stores selling nothing but furniture. Hal's encouragement always ended with John saying. 'Yeah. Sure I will, Hal. When the Broken Spur is back on a sound footing.'

Well, now John Bannion could do what he wanted most to do, and Hal would have a ranch that was debt free. From there on, it would be up to Hal to make the Broken Spur what it had been, and better, before misfortune had befallen Tom Bannion.

Hal woke to a sunrise painted by God's hand, the air crisp and clean with a soft kissing breeze to cool a man's skin. Of course it wouldn't last. As the day aged, the sun would heat the earth until it burned a man's feet to stand on it without boots, but it was the last day of the trek back to the Broken Spur, and the day that Hal Bannion had been praying for since he'd set out for Miguel Santos' ranch.

'Ain't goin' to be long now, Hal,' Ben Rogers, Hal's right hand over the long haul, said. 'Coffee?'

'Sure.'

Rogers poured from a blackened pot into the tin cup that Bannion held out, and then sat back against his saddle.

'I guess John is goin' to be mighty pleased and surprised when you drive them high-stepping beauties on to Broken Spur range, Hal.'

Bannion laughed. 'To tell you the truth, Ben, I'm going to be every bit as surprised, and even more pleased.'

Everyone in Crosby Flats, and the ranches around, knew Hal Bannion's desperate venture was a last throw of the dice for the Broken Spur, and if it did not pay off, the Bannion brothers would walk away from the Spur in only the clothes they stood up in.

Alice, Luther Bramwell's daughter, and the

woman whom Hal secretly worshipped, but who had eyes only for John Bannion, had urged Hal to accept her father's terms for the Broken Spur, or even the maggot Charles Ashby's offer.

'At least that will give you starting money, Hal,' she'd pleaded.

Hal knew she made good sense.

'It'll give John and you a chance to start on new pastures.'

'But new pastures ain't the Broken Spur,' Hal had argued.

There was other advice from Andrew Barret. 'Sell off part of the Broken Spur and refinance.'

But if a part of the ranch had to be sold, it would have to be the part with the best grass and water. Hal reckoned that such a move would doom the rest of the ranch anyway. What the hell good was a ranch with stunted grass and little water to improve matters?.

'It took a whole lotta guts to do what you've done, Hal,' Ben Rogers opined.

'I ain't done nothing yet, Ben,' Hal replied, frowning worriedly. 'Not until I've got these critters fattened on Broken Spur grass and sold to the army.' He sighed wearily. 'Then and only then will I have done something.'

'Don't sell yourself short,' Rogers chuckled. 'I figure that a year from now the Broken Spur will have bounced right back.'

Hal Bannion hoped he was right. He stood up,

pitching the dregs of his coffee on the fire. 'Best get moving.'

'You're frettin' is over, Hal,' Rogers told him as he slung the saddle on his horse. 'Nightfall will see us safely back at the Spur.'

For the last few minutes, Hal Bannion had been feeling an icy finger on his spine. Maybe his niggling fears were the product of being so close to achieving his goal, yet fearing having it grabbed from him. A natural reaction after the spell of bad luck and misfortune that had befallen him? He hoped that was all.

'OK, you layabouts,' Ben Rogers hollered. 'Time to hit the trail!' Rogers strode about rousting men from under their blankets and herding them, grumbling, round the fire for grub.

'Not more damn beans, Dan Reilly, a curly red-haired man, groused. 'I tell ya, Ben Rogers, my butt talking back to me kept me 'wake most of the night.'

'Yeah,' a smallish man groaned. 'We all heard.'

There was general good-humoured laughter round the fire.

'Thank heaven I'll be back in Crosby Flats tonight,' Frank Daley, the youngest of the men sighed. 'I sure hope the ladies committee ain't run Ruth Sullivan outa town.'

Mention of Ruth Sullivan, a redhead with cat-green eyes who was first in line when God handed out good looks, brought a collective sigh of longing from the men.

'I hear John and Ruth are real close, Hal,' Daley sniggered.

It was no secret around Crosby Flats that Hal Bannion and his brother did not see eye-to-eye on John's regular visits first to the Cat's Paw Saloon, and then to the cottage in which Ruth Sullivan entertained outside of town. Hal was a temperate man and, though he realized a town needed women like Ruth Sullivan so that decent women could be safe, he did not wholly agree with the sheriff turning a blind eye to town laws and allowing whoredom to flourish.

'Ruth is a good woman, Hal,' John Bannion had many times argued. 'A whole lot better than the righteous petticoats who'd have her run out of town.'

'You figure John'll eventually git Ruth 'tween the sheets for keeps, Hal?'

The question came from a mean-faced man with the handle of Burt Shannon, whom Hal would not have had along if he had the poke to pick and choose. He had had to take whoever would go for the pay he could offer, and he'd be the first to acknowledge that, in the main, with his meagre resources, he'd been fortunate.

'Folk wonder if it'll be Ruth or Alice Bramwell, Hal,' Shannon speculated.

'Alice has always been real sweet on John,' another man said. 'Since they were tots.'

'Old Luther Bramwell ain't sweet on John none,

though,' Shannon sniggered. I hear he's tryin' to marry Alice off to one of them fancy Dans she has on her arm now and then 'round Crosby Flats.'

Mention of Alice Bramwell's keeness for his brother sent a knife through Hal Bannion's heart. He'd been in love with Alice Bramwell since they were kids. She'd come to visit the Broken Spur, often staying over when Luther and Mrs Bramwell attended some swank ball or bash. It was always towards John that she drifted, and nothing changed as they reached adulthood. She included Hal in her invitations to town shindigs, and they'd circle and sashay, but she'd always end up with John.

The men went on to discuss the merits of both women until their comments about Alice Bramwell hiked Hal's ire to fist-delivering fury. Ben Rogers, who had been observing Bannion's growing anger, intervened in the increasingly ribald exchanges. Rogers' hand closed vice-like over Hal's wrist to stay his balled fist that he was about to launch into Burt Shannon's leering face.

In a quiet aside, Rogers said, 'Another day, Hal. If you buck one, the others might side with him and ride. You can't afford to pay such a high price. Like 'em or not, we need every man.'

Hal knew the sense of Rogers' words, but that did nothing to stem the tide of red anger that rose inside him like a rampant cancer.

'There'll be time to settle later, Hal,' Rogers

cautioned, and ordered the crew, 'Hit leather, boys.' Rogers fell in alongside Bannion and groaned. 'Damn, Hal. Why don't you go a-calling on Alice Bramwell with your heart on your sleeve and shush the wagging tongues of Crosby Flats? It's the worst kept secret in these parts that you've got a hankering for Alice Bramwell.'

'Ain't none of your business, Ben,' Bannion flared. 'I'd sure 'preciate it if everyone minded their own, instead of poking their noses into mine!'

'You know,' Rogers countered, 'Tom Bannion was an ornery old cuss, much given to liverishness when he was of a mind. I reckon he ain't ever going to be gone while you're 'round, Hal!'

The two men glared hotly at each other for a long spell before they burst into laughter. Rogers said, 'Ain't we a pair, huh, Hal Bannion!' Then, riding ahead, slung back, 'Let's get these horses to the Broken Spur.'

Hal knew his love for Alice Bramwell was known to all, and Alice was not deaf, so that had to mean that his feelings did not interest her one little bit. It was also a fact that Luther Bramwell would have neither John or his feet under his table. Alice, his only child, would, if Luther Bramwell got his way and he most likely would as always, marry one of those Southern gents like himself that Burt Shannon called fancy Dans, who'd know which fork or spoon to pick up at the swanky eateries and balls that the Bramwells frequented. Even the day before he had set out for Mexico, one of the Southern dandies was visiting with the Bramwells, Luther showing Alice off on his arm in town. There was only one consolation for Hal Bannion, and that was the uneasy look on Alice Bramwell's face as she passed by.

'Well, c'mon!' Ben Rogers' shout jolted Hal from his reverie. 'Mooning 'bout Alice Bramwell ain't going to move these critters one inch nearer the Spur.'

'I wish I was your age, Ben,' Hal said good-humouredly. 'Then there'd be no point in mooning, 'cause there wouldn't be a darn thing I could do about a chance, if I got a chance!' Hal raced ahead, robbing Rogers of the opportunity to spout the spiky riposte on his lips. He began counting the seconds to journey's end.

There was a worrying spell in the afternoon when Rogers, scouting ahead, reported four riders expressing an unhealthy interest in them, but it came to nothing and, as dusk clutched the day away with black fingers, Hal breathed easy for the first time in a long time, as Broken Spur range was reached.

'Eldorado, eh, Hal?' Ben Rogers sighed. 'Can't say that I haven't had my hairy moments along the way.'

'Me and you, Ben,' Hal Bannion sighed content-edly.

'Hope that brother of yours has got clean sheets and hot grub ready!'

Hal galloped ahead, bursting at the seams to share his good fortune with his brother, but, as he drew nearer the house, became troubled by the emptiness of the landscape and the general run-down appearance of the house and yard.

'Damn, John!' Hal swore angrily. 'You promised me new corrals. Where the hell are they?'

'Ain't going to have a single swallow while you're gone, Hal.' John Bannion's promise, which Hal had foolishly believed, rang bitterly hollow in his ears. 'I'll he much too busy getting things right for your return, to have time for supping.'

'Well,' Hal grumbled, as he hitched his horse to the rail outside the house, casting his eye over the neglect all round, 'it seems to me that your promise was worth as much as a plug nickel, Brother!' Striding angrily on to the porch, he hollered, 'John! Are you in the house?' When, a second later he found the house empty and cold, Hal sighed. 'I guess the Cat's Paw Saloon more'n likely!'

He stalked back out of the house and was about to mount his horse for the angry ride to Crosby Flats when Alice Bramwell rode up.

'Father saw you coming, Hal. He sent me over to . . . well, to. . . .'

Hal Bannion's delight on seeing Alice Bramwell was short-lived. There was pain in her blue eyes, and her agitated fingers fretted her blonde hair, the way they'd always done since she was a child and had difficult tidings to deliver.

'I know, Alice.' Hal waved his hand about. 'John's in the Cat's Paw, ain't he?'

'No!'

Hal looked about him angrily. 'Well, he's certainly not here!'

Alice's fingers fretted her hair some more.

'What is it you want to tell me, Alice,' he encouraged wearily.

'John is dead, Hal,' she blurted out tearfully.

Hal's mind spun, trying to grasp what Alice had just said. 'How can John be dead?' he wailed. 'He was waiting for me to get back. He wouldn't just up and die, Alice!'

'He didn't just up and die, Hal. . . .' Bannion's eyes bored into Alice Bramwell, dragging a full explanation out of her. 'John was shot during a poker game at the Cat's Paw.'

'A poker game?'

'He was on a binge. Got into this poker game that turned sour. John got mad and challenged the winner. Accused him of cheating.'

'Who was this winner, Alice?' Hal questioned quietly. 'Charles Ashby?'

'No. A stranger. In fact, a visiting preacher,' she said, bemused.

'A preacher?'

'The Reverend Goodwood. He's a tent preacher.

Came to town the day after you left for Mexico, Hal.'

'Did this *preacher* kill John?'

'No. Speck Spencer, the gunnie who backs all of Ashby's play did that.'

'I know Speck Spencer's role,' Hal growled with sullen anger.

'Spencer acted as the unarmed preacher's protector.'

'When did this happen, Alice?'

'A couple of days after you left!'

Hal looked into the flaming horizon as the sun died, fighting his tears. 'John said he'd be waiting for my return!' Alice Bramwell took Hal in her arms, unashamed of her tears. 'Damn it, Alice. Why did he have to go to the Cat's Paw? He promised me he wouldn't.'

'John had a weakness, Hal. That weakness made it easy for the Devil to work on him.'

'The Devil and Ashby!' Bannion snarled.

'Shush, Hal,' Alice coaxed. As he quietened, she told him, 'We buried John in the north range, near those oaks he'd always said would fill his furniture store, when he opened it in town.'

'Guess I'd best pay my respects,' Hal said bleakly.

'Hal.' He turned to face Alice as she grabbed his arm. 'There's something else you should know: the Broken Spur isn't yours any more. I guess neither are those horses.'

Hal Bannion's breath left him with a whoosh, and he staggered backwards under Alice Bramwell's hammer-blow news.

'John handed over markers on the ranch and all its assets to the Reverend Goodwood. Ashby bought them from the preacher that very night. He's the new owner of the Broken Spur, Hal. He owns every blade of grass. I got Father to check out the facts. John's marker will withstand any challenge!'

'But he was drunk!'

'At the end of a three-day bender,' Alice confirmed.

'A three-day bender!' Hal exclaimed. 'John didn't have that kind of money, Alice.'

'Seems his credit was good at the Cat's Paw.'

Bemused, Hal exclaimed, 'Ashby wouldn't give a Bannion a drink of water, Alice. Everyone knows that.'

Alice continued, 'Don't go reading in something that's not there, Hal. The Reverend Goodwood did all he could to talk sense to John. His challenge was rash. Goodwood held an unbeatable hand, that he was willing to throw in, if John backed off, but he persisted with his challenge, so the reverend suggested John give him a marker. Then John kept on giving markers until the total meant that all of the Broken Spur was on the table. John just wouldn't heed good sense. Even Ashby tried to stem his lunacy.'

'Ashby? A good Samaritan to a Bannion? That stretches belief too far, Alice.'

'The more anyone tried to talk sense to John, the more stubborn he became.'

'Is this preacher still around?'

'No. Goodwood left town that night.'

'That night! Seems to me the Reverend Goodwood was in a mighty hurry to shake off the dust of Crosby Flats.' Flint-eyed, Hal Bannion opined, 'Charles Ashby's had a mite too much good fortune for my liking, Alice.'

'Where're you headed, Hal?' Alice Bramwell enquired worriedly, as Hal Bannion leaped into the saddle.

'To see Ashby, of course!' he flung back as he thundered out of the yard, oblivious to Alice's pleas to wait until his anger abated.

Ben Rogers had to be alert and nifty to get out of the way of Hal's charging mount at the entrance to the Broken Spur, and sat looking after Hal as he galloped at full stretch along the trail to Crosby Flats.

'What in tarnation. . . ?' he mumbled.

He was just turning back on to the trail, when he again had to draw rein urgently, as Alice Bramwell chased Hal Bannion's tail as if they both had the Devil after them.

'What's gotten into them?' Frank Daley asked Rogers.

'Don't know.' Rogers joined in the chase to

Crosby Flats. 'Guess I'd better find out though.' As he charged after Hal and Alice Bramwell, he knew that there was trouble in the wind.

And big trouble at that!

THREE

Hal Bannion did not slow his charge one jot, until he kicked up dust outside the Cat's Paw Saloon. Hitting the ground running, his loping stride cleared the steps up to the saloon porch in an athletic leap, and he shouldered the batwings aside with such ferocity that they sagged on their hinges under the onslaught. Then he rolled ahead with the crowd-separating power of a locomotive right up to the table from which Charles Ashby ruled his domain.

The Cat's Paw patrons, swelled by the crowd piling in behind Hal expecting trouble, fell into a hush. Everyone was expecting Bannion's call on the saloon owner as soon as he got back from Mexico, and heard that Charles Ashby was the new owner of the Broken Spur, knowing that Hal Bannion would have preferred Satan himself to have got his hands on the ranch.

'Why, hello there, Hal,' Ashby greeted cordially. Ordering one of his sidekicks out of his chair, he invited. 'Sit.'

Hal reached across the table, grabbed Ashby by his fancy silk shirt and hauled him across the table to glare him eyeball to eyeball.

'Easy, Speck,' Ashby ordered Spencer, his protector, as the gunslinger's hand dived for the pearl-handled Colt .45 on his right hip; a gun that had despatched many a man to his Maker. 'I think Mr Bannion's reaction, under the circumstances, is understandable, don't you?' His raised voice took in the crowd and brought a sympathetic mumble.

'I'm going to kill you where you stand, Ashby,' Hal growled.

Speck Spencer's hand again hovered over his pistol. 'This fella's a real fire-cracker, boss. I think you should let me punch his ticket before he becomes a nuisance.'

Ashby smiled his snake-oil smile. 'I can handle this, Speck. Like I said, Hal's reaction is understandable, with him grieving for his brother. Why don't we sit and talk,' he crooned. 'Let these good folk get back to their pleasures.'

Alice Bramwell's eruption through the batwings tested the hinges again, and offered the Cat's Paw patrons another diversion.

'Let's go home, Hal,' she pleaded.

'No! Not until I've finished my business with Ashby.'

'I'll go home with ya, honey doll,' a lanky drunk standing near Alice Bramwell offered, and earned a jaw buster from one of Luther Bramwell's rannies for his drunken boldness, that skittered him across the floor to crash his head against a brass spittoon. He got up, but before the ranny could follow through, fell back to the floor, unconscious. Instantly, two of Ashby's hardcases dragged the drunk to the door and kicked him out.

'May I offer my apologies for that man's brazen suggestion, Miss Bramwell,' Ashby said.

The excitement was just dying down when it was hiked again by Ben Rogers' arrival, and this time one of the batwings gave up and fell to the floor, shattered.

'My,' Ashby hummed. 'Isn't this a night for callers.'

Laughter washed around the saloon, but was quickly ended as Hal Bannion's fist crunched against Charles Ashby's mouth. This time Speck Spencer's gun flashed in his hand and Ashby did not intervene.

'Put it back in its sheath, Spencer!' Ben Rogers ordered, gun already cocked. 'This argument is between Ashby and Hal. So let's keep our noses out of it.'

Spencer smirked, 'It's you've got the cocked gun, Rogers.'

Ben Rogers placed his gun out of reach on the bar top. 'I ain't got a gun any more, Spencer.'

Spencer, under the gaze of the crowd, resisted the temptation to lay Rogers low. Idiot that he was for taking such a chance, it was all he deserved. Parting with his gun was not in Speck Spencer's nature, but he was left with no choice when Sheriff Ed Bradley threw aside the remaining batwing, shotgun hoisted. His glance went to Ashby on the floor, mouth bloodied, Hal Bannion standing over him ready to finish what he'd started.

'Back off, Hal,' Bradley ordered. 'You too, Spencer.' Then his flinty grey eyes swept the lurking ragbag of Ashby hardcases. 'That goes for you, too, boys. Slide your guns my way.'

Ashby struggled up. 'This is none of my doing, Sheriff Bradley. Bannion came through the place like a twister, bent on trouble.'

Bradley's gaze settled on Hal Bannion. 'Is it as Mr Ashby says, Hal?'

'I guess,' he conceded. 'But I ain't full of steam for nothing, Ed.'

Bradley's grey eyes locked with Bannion's fiery amber. 'I guess you've got a right to be mad as hell, Hal, but it ain't Mr Ashby who you should be mad at. John was loco to do what he did, but it was his own doing.'

Bannion's pointed finger shot out in Charles Ashby's direction, and he asked Bradley in disbelief, 'Are you backing this sidewinder, Ed?'

'Ain't a matter of taking sides,' the sheriff said curtly, ticked off that Hal should have taken an accusatory tone for no good reason that he could see. 'Like I told you, Hal, it's a matter of right. The fact is, Mr Ashby is now the legal and rightful owner of the Broken Spur, and everything that goes with it.'

'I never gave my say-so,' Bannion grumbled.

'You didn't have to: John was the legal owner of the Broken Spur, and it was his right to gamble it away if he was of a mind to.'

Hal Bannion felt a familiar gall burn in his gut. He had never figured out why Tom Bannion had seen fit to hand over the Broken Spur lock, stock and barrel to John, who had little interest in ranching, instead of him who wanted nothing else. Folk had said that his head was sick when he did so. That's as maybe, but now his loco decision meant that Hal was out of house and home, and penniless.

'I don't want your ranch, Hal,' Ashby said, raising his voice for all to hear. 'I'm a saloon keeper, not a rancher.'

Hal's hope was stirred. Was it possible that Charles Ashby had a decent streak in him after all?

'You'll return John's markers?'

Ashby shrugged his elegantly clad shoulders and ran his delicate, work-shy fingers along his black pencil moustache. 'Sure I will, but I'm a businessman, Hal, that you've got to understand!' His eyes swept the saloon. 'I paid top dollar for your brother's markers. I just can't hand them over for nothing. Of course, I won't charge a dime over what I paid for them.'

Bannion knew that his hope for a show of decency from Ashby had been misplaced.

'You can have the Broken Spur back if you can meet what I paid the Reverend Goodwood for it. That's fair, isn't it?' Ashby's gaze drifted across a sea of nodding heads. 'I'd be forsaking a very hefty profit. The Broken Spur is a spread with real potential, but it's got more still now that's it's got all those fine horses on its range!'

'Seems fair to me,' Speck Spencer shouted. 'Mr Ashby is being real generous, ain't that so, folks?'

Ashby's entourage led the cheering.

Ed Bradley, knowing Hal's lack of resources, as did Ashby, sighed heavily.

'You know I ain't got the poke to buy my brother's markers right off, Ashby,' Hal grated.

'Sorry to hear that, Hal,' he sympathized, 'but you can't expect me to just throw away a valuable asset, now can you?'

Hal knew he had no cards to play.

'You saw John's markers, Ed?' Hal said to Bradley.

The sheriff confirmed it. 'I asked Mr Ashby to show me them that very night, Hal, right after the ruckus. John was waving a gun about wildly. As I heard it, he could have shot half-a-dozen people. Spencer was within his rights, I reckon. He gave John every chance to sheath his iron before he plugged him.'

'John was cheated, Ed,' Hal raged, and then raised his voice to a shout. 'You all know that Ashby's got no love for a Bannion, and has always coveted the Broken Spur.'

'It was legal, that I can tell, Hal,' Bradley said emphatically. 'Now go home.'

'Home?' Bannion challenged. 'Where would that be, Sheriff?'

'You're welcome to stay here at the Cat's Paw,' Ashby invited Hal, 'for as long as it takes to get your affairs in order.'

'I'd rather board with the Devil, Ashby,' Bannion spat.

Ben Rogers came forward. 'There's nothing you can do, Hal, much as you want to. The Broken Spur is gone and you'll have to live with that.'

'Tell you what, Hal,' Ashby crooned, his snake smile back on his lips. 'I'll hold off moving on to the Broken Spur for a spell, a week, maybe even two, to give you the chance to buy back John's markers. Meantime, if you can raise the cash, you just mosey along here to the Cat's Paw and we'll close the deal.'

Angered by Ashby's insincere offer, Hal went for his throat with the ferocity of a mountain cat, and would have ripped it out if the combined strength of Ben Rogers and Ed Bradley had not hauled him off the saloon owner. Both men manhandled Hal out of the saloon, kicking and fighting, with Ashby's taunt of, 'Poor, Hal,' ringing in his ears.

Outside the saloon, Bradley warned, 'It's over,

Hal. I won't stand for you making mayhem for Ashby, when there ain't no grounds for doing so, you hear?'

Hal Bannion flared hotly, 'If you're on Ashby's side, Sheriff, you share Ashby's risks!'

'Are you threatening me, Hal?' Bradley asked, equally angry.

Dourly, Bannion restated, 'Like I said, Sheriff, if you're on Ashby's side, you share Ashby's risks.'

Attempting to reason with him, Bradley said, 'It ain't my choice, Hal. Like it or not, the law's on Ashby's side in this, and it don't matter what you or me think of his ways of doing things. In this matter, there ain't no challenge to be made.'

Wearily, he offered, 'I can offer you a cell in the town jail if you've got no place else to bed down.'

'I could ask my father to—'

'I won't be beholden, Alice,' Hal said, cutting her offer short, 'but I thank you.' Then, turning to Ed Bradley, his fire burned out. 'I'll be glad of your hospitality, Ed, until I can straighten out my thoughts.'

As Hal settled down for the night in the town jail, the sheriff said, 'I hope this wrangle with Ashby is over and done with, Hal.'

Grimly, Hal Bannion answered, 'Ed, you and me know that Ashby is as crooked as a snake's slither. It's my guess that John was cheated and set up for killing, and I aim to get back what's mine.'

Bradley's face stiffened. 'I told you, Hal. I saw

John's markers, and there are witnesses who say that the Reverend Goodwood did everything he could to curb your brother's foolishness, as did Ashby. John wouldn't listen. You know yourself how muleheaded he could be when he was liquored up.'

'Muleheaded, granted, Ed, but even if John was crazy enough to gamble away the Broken Spur, he would never be loco enough to go up against Speck Spencer, even with a barrel of rot-gut in his belly!'

'No knowing what a man will do when he's fired up by whiskey, Hal. There's nothing like whiskey to twist a man's reasoning.'

Hal Bannion eyed Bradley with a level gaze. 'Strange, don't you think. . . .'

'What is?'

'A fire-and-brimstone preacher like the Reverend Goodwood in a poker game?'

Ed Bradley's face crumpled in thought. 'Now that you bring it up, I thought it a little strange myself. Then again, if Goodwood fancied a little poker, there ain't no law against a preacher playing cards.'

'What if Goodwood was Ashby's agent in swindling John, Ed. Who'd suspect a cheating preacher?'

'That's loco talk, Hal. You're clutching at straws. My advice is to accept John's foolishness and start over. Only yesterday, Luther Bramwell was in town hiring, and down the road—'

'Down the road, nothing, Ed,' Bannion cut in angrily. 'On the low wages Luther Bramwell pays,

I'd have a beard down to my toes before I'd get enough together to start over.'

'Work your cards right and everything that Bramwell owns could fall right into your lap, Hal.'

'Don't say another word, Ed,' Hal cautioned. 'I ain't the kind of man who lives off a woman, or the dead!'

Ed Bradley sighed resignedly, before stating, 'However this works out between you and Ashby, I want to make one thing arrow straight with you, Hal Bannion: there can be no favours. Ashby is within his rights to own the Broken Spur.'

'I ain't asking for no favours,' Hal growled. 'I'll try not to be a guest for too long.'

'Stay as long as you have to, Hal.'

Ed Bradley exited the cells, closing behind him the door leading to the sheriff's office. His demeanour was weary. He didn't like the idea of Hal Bannion losing the Broken Spur to the Cat's Paw owner, but in his twenty-three years as a peace officer he'd never once sold out to any interest, and he'd be damned if he'd start now, only a few months from his pension. Tom Bannion and he were among the first in the wagon and tent town that had grown into Crosby Flats, and it grieved him to have to back Ashby against Hal Bannion, but he had no choice and that was that!

If Hal Bannion caused mayhem he'd deal with it.

FOUR

Hal slept fitfully. Jaded from the tension and sheer hard work of the drive from Mexico, he should have slept the sleep of the dead. Instead, his dreams tossed him all night, and he woke unrefreshed and even more troubled than when he had lain down the night before.

'You look like week-old shit!' Ed Bradley remarked, as he ushered in a piping hot breakfast from the café across the street from the law office. Though Hal's mouth watered at the sight of bacon and eggs, his pride stopped his saliva in its tracks.

'I ain't a prisoner, Ed.'

'So?'

'So, I ain't entitled.'

'The town ain't forking out for this,' Bradley informed him, and in response to Bannion's raised eyebrows, explained: 'Alice Bramwell left word with Cissie Clark, the owner of the Knife and

Fork, that your feeding needs should be taken care of.'

'I ain't no charity case neither!' Hal declared spiritedly.

'No? All you've got is what you stand up in, Hal Bannion. So have sense and be grateful for the kindness shown you by a good and fine woman.'

'Give it any handle that comes to mind, Ed: in my book, it's charity, and I ain't filling my belly with charity grub!'

'What is it about you Bannion boys?' Bradley growled. 'Were you born with rocks for brains?'

'I'll use your facilities out back, Ed,' Bannion said stiffly, 'then I'll be on my way.'

'You ain't got a red cent. Where're you going to go?'

'Don't rightly know yet,' Hal smiled, 'but I hope it'll be some place where I'm not preached at all the time.'

'Hank Daniels is looking for help.'

'Daniels? You mean Daniels' general store?'

'Only one Hank Daniels in town that I know of,' Bradley said, his impatience showing at the scoff in Hal Bannion's tone. 'Got a job for ya.'

'Doing what?'

'Clerking and general handiness.'

Hal snorted. 'I ain't no store clerk, Ed, I'm a rancher!'

'Without a ranch,' the sheriff reminded Hal brusquely, 'a belly to fill and a body to clothe.' He shoved the tray at Bannion. 'Eat your damn breakfast, you stubborn cuss!'

'No.'

'God dang it,' Bradley grated and stormed back to his office, shaking the building with the slam of the connecting door to the cells, 'ain't pride Satan's tool for sure!'

Hal shaved and washed in the outside privy behind the jail, finding the frosty chill of the water refreshing and head clearing. He looked at himself in the cracked mirror that Bradley had lent him, and asked himself, 'Where to now, Hal Bannion? You ain't got money; no place to rest your head other than the jail, and you owe Miguel Santos big time. You're a pretty sorry lot, ain't you?'

He'd thought long and hard during the sleepless night about Ed Bradley's warning about bucking Charles Ashby's right to the Broken Spur and, much as it soured him, he had to admit that if John had been a fool, he would have to pay the price. He could rant all he liked, but it wouldn't change a thing; Ashby would still be sitting pretty. How was he to meet his debt to Miguel Santos? There was only one way, get a job and work hard, but the only one hiring around Crosby Flats was Luther Bramwell. He wouldn't even consider clerking for Hank Daniels, and asking Bramwell for a job after the bust up the year before about strays, would surely choke him. He probably wouldn't hire him on anyway. If Alice did the asking, old Luther would listen, but that was charity with a capital C, and he'd rather curl up and die than be on the receiving end of any man's charity, most of all Luther Bramwell's!

The argument about strays was not the real issue between the Broken Spur and the Big B: that was about Bramwell slinging the Big B brand over the Bannion spread, the same as he'd done with most of his neighbours. Luther Bramwell was a man with strong predatory instincts, and ravenous ambition.

'The only thing that will stop the boundaries of the Big B spreading will be the Rio Grande,' was the commonly held view of Bramwell's ambition to eventually own every blade of grass in Texas.

Hal Bannion's thoughts turned to Charles Ashby, and the true reason for the saloon owner's grabbing of the Broken Spur sprang gallingly to mind. He'd have only one use for it and that would be as a trading chip to get Alice Bramwell on his arm and into his bed. Business made for strange bedfellows, and Luther Bramwell, cold-hearted bastard that he was, would, Hal reckoned, not hesitate to trade his daughter's happiness by accepting Charles Ashby as a son-in-law, to gain the prize of the Broken Spur.

There was another reason, too, why getting his hands on the Spur would sweeten the saloon-owner's dreams, and that was revenge. John

Bannion, a woman-attracting man if ever there was one, had taken Ellie Benton from Ashby. Ellie, a local trader's daughter, had been Ashby's route into Crosby Flats' society, with the plus of having one of the town's finest women to warm his nights, until one day, John Bannion took to sweet-talking her, and from that second on Ashby was out of the picture. Folk had heard Ashby swear to even the score with John and, by having him killed and getting his hands on the Broken Spur, too, Hal reckoned he had.

Bannion figured that Ashby had also vented his spleen on Ellie Benton. The Broken Spur was being readied for John and Ellie's wedding, when Ellie was the victim of an unknown assassin, hired John and Hal believed, by the ditched and jealous Charles Ashby. Everyone, including Ed Bradley, had put the Bannions' accusations about Ashby's involvement in Ellie Benton's murder down to the bad blood that was between them.

It was after Ellie Benton's murder that whiskey became John's preferred sedation, a choice that had finally handed the prize of the Broken Spur to the man he hated most.

Before Hal Bannion stepped out of the law office, Ed Bradley repeated his warning that, as far as he was concerned, Charles Ashby owned the Broken Spur fair and square and Hal was to give that gent a wide berth and no grief.

The warning did nothing to sweeten Hal's

humour. He charged out of the sheriff's office with a gripe-ridden scowl, and almost knocked Ruth Sullivan over the hitch rail outside the office, grabbing her only at the last second as her petticoats flared and her legs went every which way.

'I'm real sorry, ma'am,' Hal apologized, righting Ruth before recognizing her. When he saw that it was Ruth Sullivan, his face iced over and his hands fled from her waist as if he'd just picked up a rattler.

'Accidents happen, Hal,' Ruth said quietly. 'Sorry about John.'

'Ma'am.' Hal's tone was unfriendly.

'Your brother was a kind man!'

'And a hundred fools, too!' Hal grated.

'Well, best he getting along if I'm to catch the stage. Goodbye, Hal.'

' 'Bye,' he mumbled.

As she walked away, Hal became acutely conscious of how lacking in Christian spirit his attitude had been to Ruth Sullivan, since the first day she'd arrived in Crosby Flats a year ago. Well, what attitude was he supposed to have towards a woman who entertained what she euphemistically called *male friends* – one of whom had been his brother?

A lot of folk, including a high proportion of the town's men who had visited Ruth Sullivan, had campaigned for her banishment, and a whole passel of those hypocrites would weep now that she was leaving town.

Ruth had moved out of the Cat's Paw six months before to a small cottage about a mile outside of town, where she received callers – and there were plenty – but only on the nights that John Bannion would not be calling. When his brother chose, he had Ruth Sullivan's exclusive attention.

'Prudence Shankley's finally got her way,' Ed Bradley said, coming to stand in the law-office door, his grey eyes reflecting his appreciation of Ruth Sullivan's gait, as she made her way along the boardwalk to the stage depot. 'Damn fine woman,' he opined unashamedly and, responding to Hal's open, but unvoiced criticism, 'Come on, Hal. You've got to admit that Ruth Sullivan would have a corpse randy in a second flat.'

'In my opinion,' Hal intoned loftily, 'the town owes a great deal to Prudence Shankley for her insistence that Ruth Sullivan should offer her favours in another town!'

'Jeez, Hal,' Bradley chuckled. 'You've got more starch in you than Yang's Laundry!' Then, winking broadly and elbowing Hal playfully, he enquired, 'Are you telling me that you never flattened feathers with Ruth Sullivan, Hal?' His chuckle deepened. ''Cause if you are, then you must be the only man around here who ain't!'

'You're supposed to uphold the law, Ed,' Hal Bannion accused stiffly.

'You know what,' Bradley said, sighing heavily, 'I often wonder how you and John came out of the same womb, Hal.' Before slamming the law-office door shut, he reminded Bannion, 'There's a bed here tonight if you want it. That is if you can stand sleeping under the same roof with a sinful heathen like me.'

It wasn't the first time that someone had pondered on the difference between John and him, the proverbial chalk and cheese. But Hal had his way of seeing things and he had a right to his opinions. John Bannion liked women, liquor and poker in that order, until whiskey more or less sidelined the other two after Ellie Benton's demise.

'You'd have me a saint, Hal!' had often been John Bannion's chortling riposte to Hal's pleas to temper his ways. 'A man's got a mouth to drink whiskey, hands to hold cards and' – at this point John Bannion's smile would become positively leery – 'lips to kiss gals with.' Before heading back to town for a night's rousting, he would add, 'It's the order of things, Hal, and I'll be damned if I could walk the righteous paths that you walk, Brother!'

'You'll have to pay the Devil his due sooner or later, John!' Hal would scold him.

Glumly, Bannion strode away along the boardwalk in stalking steps that he suddenly realized did not have any place to go except the livery where his horse was stabled. He decided to ride out to John's grave to pay his respects. Alice Bramwell had told him he'd find it in the shade of the mighty oaks, from where John often hauled wood to make his furniture. It was his favourite spot on Broken Spur range, and Hal reckoned he owed Alice Bramwell his good wishes and kind thoughts for arranging to have John planted where he'd have wanted to be.

The morning, though favoured with a bright sun had a chill to it as Fall chased summer away. Hal, once free of the confines of Crosby Flats, town life not agreeing with him much, began to enjoy the ride across the edge of Luther Bramwell's Big B range, then along Devil's Creek, a strange monicker for a restful haven, and on to the familiar range of the Broken Spur. On cresting a ridge north of the ranch house, his breath caught in his throat on seeing the grazing horses in the valley below, horses that were to make the Broken Spur a respected ranch again, but would now go to fatten Charles Ashby's bank account.

'Hell, John,' he cried out in anguished anger, 'why'd you have to break your promise to me!' He was instantly sorry for his spiteful outburst. All the signs were, according to Alice Bramwell, that John had fought his weakness tooth and nail before succumbing to the Devil's coaxing.

He let his horse set its own easy pace down from the ridge, across the meadow and down the dip to the creek and the stand of oak that had been John Bannion's special place since childhood.

Entering the wooded creek, Hal's heart tightened on seeing the mound of fresh earth adorned with a bouquet of the wild flowers that grew abundantly along the sun-favoured creek. A rough wooden cross of two tree branches tied with the green ribbon much favoured by Alice Bramwell, stood at the head of the grave, the ribbon fluttering in the gentle breeze that whispered ghostly through the trees.

Hal removed his hat and knelt. He prayed, but not in a formal way. He spoke of times past and times future.

'Don't know what lies ahead for me, John,' he murmured, 'but I reckon times won't be easy. I've got Miguel Santos' slate to wipe clean, and that's going to take a whole lot of hard work to accomplish. Then there'll be a place of my own to get.'

Hal Bannion was suddenly wearier than he'd ever been. 'That'll take more back-breaking work.' Then, conscious of how his brother must be hearing his words, went on, 'I ain't placing no blame on you, John. I know you did your best, and that's all a man can do.' Bitterness tainted his voice. 'I know that scoundrel Ashby cheated you, John, and sooner or later I aim to square acounts with that hobo.'

The crack of a twig behind Hal alerted him to

company, the creeping kind. He spun around, hand poised over his pistol. The sneer on Speck Spencer's lips was one of pure evil.

'You're trespassin' on Ashby range, Bannion!'

The equally evil man backing Spencer, Skeet Blayney, sniggered. 'Would you say that that was a rope-slingin' offence, Speck?'

'Ashby's gotta right to protect his prop'ty from driftin' no-goods, I reckon,' Spencer growled.

'I ain't a drifter and I ain't a no-good,' Hal grated. He shifted his stance. 'Any man who says I am better be ready to back his words.'

Speck Spencer's sneer deepened. 'Fine with me, Bannion.' His hand drifted to the Colt that hugged his hip, in a holster that was shiny from use. 'You go right ahead.' He glanced to his side-kick. 'You're a witness, Skeet. You seen how Bannion challenged me?'

'Sure did, Speck,' Blayney said, and enquired of Hal, 'You want we should plant you 'longside yer whiskey-guzzlin' brother, Bannion?'

'Heck, dunno if we can make that promise, Skeet,' Spencer cackled. 'Mr Ashby mightn't take none to havin' his prop'ty with Bannion bones all over the place.'

'Are you done with mouthing off, Spencer?' Bannion grated.

'Ready when you are, Bannion,' the gunslinger snarled.

Hal, though not regretting his challenge, had

enough brains to know that his reaction to Speck Spencer's baiting had been rash and would probably, in the next couple of seconds, send him winging to his Maker. He was no gunman, and no match for Ashby's gun-handy trouble-stirrer, whose gun-slickness was more than proven by the coffins he filled. It was a town joke that Speck Spencer put so much business the undertaker's way, any man falling to his lead got planted at a discount rate.

'Looks to me yer goin' to die of old age, Speck,' Skeet Blayney snorted, ' 'fore Bannion here gets up the steam to go fer iron.'

Laughing, Spencer gave a theatrical yawn. 'If I fall 'sleep be sure to wake me, Skeet.'

Blayney gave an even bigger yawn. 'If'n I'm still 'wake m'self, Speck.'

Hal Bannion knew he was in trouble. He could handle a gun as good as the next man, but it wasn't his trade, as it was Spencer's. He hadn't the beating of Spencer, and all he could do was hope for a miracle. Maybe he'd get lucky. Though the way his luck had been panning out lately, he wouldn't count on it.

Bannion's hand was diving for iron when a rifle shot buzzed Speck Spencer. Skeet Blayney glared angrily at Alice Bramwell emerging from the trees behind Hal, smoke trickling from the barrel of the Winchester she held. The rifle swung to cover Blayney, as his fingers curled round his pistol.

'I wouldn't do that if I were you!' Alice warned.

Skeet Blayney's rat eyes sized up his chances and decided that the odds were not in his favour. The gunman's hand went limp. 'We got no gripe with you, Miss Bramwell, ma'am.'

'I'm trespassing the same as Hal.'

'Ain't the same. You ain't a Bannion. Ashby don't want no Bannions on his range.' Blayney smiled slyly. ' 'Ceptin' those that can't walk 'way.'

Hal, fists balled, bore down on Blayney. He yanked him out of the saddle and landed a jaw-buster that sent the gunnie cartwheeling backwards. The Ashby hard case came off the ground, snarling, gun in hand. Hal kicked the pistol from his grasp and added another pile-driver to the side of Blayney's head that rattled his brain. He got dizzily to his knees, only to be floored by a final, energy-sapping side-winder that left him breathless on the ground, and Hal's shoulder throbbing painfully, but his pleasure at having whipped Blayney was a sweet compensation for his discomfort.

Alice Bramwell's rifle had swung Spencer's way to prevent his intervention in Hal Bannion's chastisement of his partner.

'On your way, Spencer,' she ordered, 'and take your friend with you.'

'And if I don't?' he snarled.

'I'll shoot you where you stand,' Alice promised stonily.

'Yeah?' Spencer sneered. 'Don't believe you have the salt, Miss Bramwell.'

Unfazed, Alice said, 'I'll count to three, Spencer. If you're still here then, you'll find out how much salt I've got.'

Skeet Blayney hauled himself shakily to his feet. 'Let's ride, Speck,' he mumbled thickly, his face already puffing up after Bannion's battering. 'There'll be 'nother time and way to settle this.'

'You scared, Skeet?' Spencer growled.

'A man who argues with a cocked gun is a fool, Speck,' Blayney said surlily.

'That's sound advice that you should heed, Spencer,' Alice opined.

Riled by Spencer's challenge, his pride dented by Alice Bramwell's intervention, Hal Bannion was in a dangerous frame of mind, the kind that makes a man over-reach himself and land in all sorts of trouble.

'This is between me and Spencer,' Hal growled. His eyes flashed Alice Bramwell's way. 'I thank you kindly, Alice, but you'll understand that a man has to fight his own corner.'

'Even if it means dying, Hal?' Alice questioned. 'Because, Hal Bannion, that's surely going to be the outcome of this uneven contest. You're a rancher, not a gun-slick.'

Skeet Blayney's courage was boosted by Hal opting to stand alone against Spencer. It would be a no-contest fight and he would be on the right side to ingratiate himself with Charles Ashby.

'One plumb centre of his pump, Speck,' he now encouraged, 'to rid us of this Bannion brood once and fer all.'

'Mebbe through the forehead, Skeet,' Spencer grinned. 'That way some sense might get into this dumb bastard's skull. 'Sides, there ain't nothin' up there nohow to damage.'

Blayney joined Spencer in a wild burst of taunting laughter.

'I swear,' Alice Bramwell warned, 'you fellas move an eyelid and I'll send you winging to Hell.'

'Damnit it, Alice,' Bannion swore. 'I told you: this is my fight, and mine alone!'

Spencer's laughter died and his eyes became chips of ice. 'Bannion's right, Miss Bramwell. You'd best be getting on home now, ma'am.'

Alice's stubborn stance hardened even more. 'Hal Bannion, I aim to save your skin, even if you have no interest in doing so yourself.' And, turning her full, glaring attention on Spencer and Blayney, chanted, 'I'm not stirring one inch, until you fellas hit the trail.'

'Alice—'

'No, Hal,' she interjected. 'I'm not going to let you throw your life away.'

'It's my life, ain't it?' he retorted huffily.

'That's true,' Alice conceded, 'but right now I reckon you're not thinking straight enough to decide on what you want to do with it, so I'm staying put.' She turned steely-blue eyes on the Ashby no-goods. 'My promise holds, gents. Move and I'll cut you down.' Shrewdly judging Blayney's shifty character, she vowed, 'You first, Blayney.'

Skeet Blayney, the ground again shifting under him, went milk white as the blood drained from his face to his toes. His tongue licked lips that were as dry as Mojave sand. It was with gut-churning relief that he heard Spencer hee-haw.

'He ain't worth the killin', Skeet. Any fella who has to hide behind a petticoat ain't far enough away from his momma's milk to be called a man.'

Relieved, Skeet Blayney cackled, 'Guess you're right at that, Speck.' Turning to Hal Bannion, he said, 'You run 'long now with the pretty lady.' His laughter reached new mocking heights. 'You pet him real good, Miss Bramwell, afore your daddy blows him to Kingdom Come fer dallying with his daughter.'

Speck Spencer strolled to his horse, arms flapping, neck craning like a pecking chicken, cutting loose with a croaky squawk that grated on Bannion's nerves.

'This ain't done with,' Hal promised the Ashby duo. 'We've got a score to even.'

They rode off, Blayney gleefully taking up Spencer's mockery. Hal's anger turned on Alice Bramwell. 'Thanks for nothing, Alice. In this country, a man needs to be able to hold his head up. Have you got any ideas on how I'm going to do that after what's just happened?'

'You're alive, Hal,' Alice countered hotly. 'That's always better than being dead.'

'Is it?' Hal groaned.

As he reached leather, back rigid with anger, Alice pleaded, 'Come back with me to the Big B, Hal. Talk to my father.'

'No.'

'He'll help. I just know he will,' Alice said in desperation.

'The Bannions and Luther Bramwell have burned their bridges, Alice.'

'You were once good friends and Christian neighbours,' Alice persisted.

'Ain't no going back,' Hal stated stubbornly.

'You're just being muleheaded, Hal Bannion! You need work; the Big B's got all the work you can handle. You can't fill your belly on old feuds.'

'I ain't going to crawl to your pa, Alice,' he grated.

Frustated, Alice spat, 'If you'd accepted his fair price for the Broken Spur, John wouldn't be lying in the cold earth, and you wouldn't be a penniless hobo!' Her outburst over, anger spent, and pained by the hurting nature of her tirade, Alice immediately apologized. 'I'm sorry, Hal. Don't you go taking any notice of my blabbering mouth.'

When he spoke, Bannion's tone was sombre. 'You spoke good sense, Alice.' His amber eyes held hers. 'But I reckon I've had enough of the Bramwells for one day.'

Alice watched Hal ride into the distance across the grass-rich range, her heart yearning and breaking. Had Hal Bannion any brains? Couldn't he see that she'd always been in love with him and not his brother? Her heart was and always had been, Hal Bannion's, ever since that first day he'd carried her books home from school, but she could never get up enough courage to tell him so, and every time she tried, her tongue stopped working.

She'd been a regular caller to the Broken Spur when times were cordial between the Bramwells and the Bannions, and she'd always ended up with John Bannion, while aching for Hal. Everyone had assumed that it was John Bannion who figured most in her thoughts, but the more easily befriended John made it possible for her to be close to his quieter brother, whom she prayed would realize where her true feelings lay; but he never had, and she never said, and both went on thinking the wrong thoughts.

Time was running out. She was heading into spinsterhood, and she was finding it more difficult to resist her father's attempts at match-making. Sooner or later, he'd push, and she'd end up shackled to one of the dandies who filled the places at their dinner-table. A daughter on the shelf was not something that Luther Bramwell would tolerate.

'Damn you to Hades for your blindness, Hal Bannion!' she swore spiritedly, and rode Midnight, the high-kicking stallion she was astride, back to the Big B at a breakneck gallop.

Hal watched Alice's south-bound sprint for the Big B, and fretted that she'd take a tumble, but he need have no fear; Alice Bramwell was better on a horse than most men, and the feisty stallion knew when he had a rider in the saddle who'd take none of his antics.

'Careful, Alice,' Hal murmured, knowing that if she did take a fall his heart would thunder to a stop. Not for the first time, he cursed his lack of courage for not telling Alice Bramwell of how she filled his dreams and had done so since that first day he'd carried her books home from school. It had always been John she'd hankered after, not him. Every time she'd visited the Broken Spur, it was to his brother she'd given her company.

'It's your own damn fault, keeping your trap shut the way you have,' flint-faced, he grumbled. 'Best put any notions you have about ever enjoying Alice Bramwell's favour right out of your silly skull! 'Sides, you ain't got two nickels to scrape together.'

The next day, he'd set out for Miguel Santos' ranch to tell him what had happened. He'd ask for a job and work off his debt to the Mexican. His debt cleared, whenever, he'd head on up to the Canadian border. He'd heard that a man could earn a crust panning for gold in the mountain streams up that way, and maybe even strike it rich.

He'd lingered, and by the time he reached Crosby Flats, night was a breath away. He scraped together enough to get his horse feed and shelter for another night. He exited the livery to a deserted, wind-blown Main, the spiteful nature of the evening having driven folk indoors. He'd be glad, he concluded, to see the back of Crosby Flats.

FIVE

'Have you got a bed for the night, Hal?' Bannion started at Ed Bradley's sudden appearance from the shadowed door of the hardware store, putting the finishing fire to a smoke cupped in his hands to protect it against the waspish wind that had picked up. 'I ain't offering charity, just the use of town facilities to which, as a citizen, you're entitled.' On seeing that Bradley's offer of hospitality was the act of a kind and good man, Hal's initial hostility to the sheriff's question vanished. 'I've got hot coffee on the stove and apple pie.'

They strolled together towards the law office, unaware of watching eyes further along the street, Bradley drawing pleasurably on the strong Mex weed that he favoured. Observing Hal's twitching nostrils, he laughed and conceded, 'Smells like crowshit, don't it?'

Passing the alley that ran alongside the bank,

they paused at the sound of whimpering. The lawman peered into the gloom that drew a curtain over the alley. 'Who's there?'

The whimpering turned to a low moan.

'You stay here, Hal,' Bradley instructed, 'but come running if needs be.' He went to the edge of the alley and, letting his glance slide round the corner, called, 'Hello in the alley. . . .'

No answer came back.

Bradley eased his pistol from its sheath and stepped into the alley with the light-footedness of a ghost. Hal grew more and more edgy as the sheriff went deeper into the alley, eaten up by the gloom until he became a shadow among shadows.

Despite the chill wind, Hal began to sweat.

There was a sudden flash that punctured a hole in the alley's gloom. The thunder of a gun rolled out of the alley. Drawing iron, Bannion hugged the bank wall, going deeper into the alley. He only saw the shadow out of the corner of his eye a split-second before his skull rocked from the blow of a gun butt, and the world curled in around him.

Freezing water brought Hal to. In the glow of torchlight, angry faces came and went, before strong hands hauled him up and he heard the words, 'Let's string the murderin' bastard up right now.'

It was a mighty popular suggestion. There was only one dissenting voice, and Hal had an advocate he'd never thought he'd have.

Charles Ashby.

'Hold on, boys. I know murder is a dirty business that angers decent citizens, and the murder of our sheriff' – Ed Bradley was dead! 'calls for swift justice, but Hal Bannion, like any other man, is entitled to a fair and just trial.'

Charles Ashby was saving his hide. The world became a stranger place by the second.

'First we need law to make a trial legal and proper. I nominate Speck Spencer to be temporary sheriff until the town council can arrange an election.

Spencer, sheriff? What next? Hal wondered if he had died and gone to Hell.

Ashby's proposal got unanimous support.

'Bring the prisoner along to the jail, Sheriff,' Ashby ordered Spencer. 'You can take your oath of office when you get there.'

There was no shortage of willing hands to drag Hal to jail. He fought to get his wits together. Someone had murdered Ed Bradley and it looked like he was in the frame for the crime.

'I didn't murder Sheriff Bradley,' he protested.

'You'll get your say in court tomorrow, Hal,' Ashby said, his devil's eyes mocking.

A beer-laden man leaned forward to land a punch on the side of Bannion's head.

'We'll have law and order here.' Ashby beckoned Skeet Blayney forward to knuckle crack the man with the barrel of his .45. 'Like I said, Hal

Bannion is entitled to a fair trial and that's what he's going to get.'

'We're wastin' time, Mr Ashby,' another man argued. 'The new sheriff saw Bannion standin' over the marshal's body with a smoking gun in his mitt. We've got the evidence to hang Bannion right now.'

Hal shook his head to loosen the cobwebs. 'I was slugged and dragged into the alley.'

Speck Spencer said, `You're as guilty as Satan himself, Bannion. And you're going to swing fer your mangey deed.'

Bannion broke Spencer's grip and pushed him aside. 'See?' he argued, parting the hair on the right side of his head, just above his right ear. 'This bump just didn't come up by itself.'

The men who were not Ashby lackies, looked to the Cat's Paw owner and his sidekicks for an explanation.

'That's a sizeable bump, sure enough,' said a man who stepped forward to examine Hal's head.

Another challenged Ashby's version of events directly. 'Looks like Hal has a case, Ashby, when he says he was slugged and dragged into the alley.'

Skeet Blayney came to his employer's rescue. 'I put that lump on Bannion's head, gents.'

'Don't doubt it none, Blayney,' the man who'd challenged Ashby chuckled. 'Question is, how, where and when?'

As he spun his lie, Skeet Blayney brazenly eye-balled Hal. 'As he stood over Sheriff Bradley's dead body. That's the how, where, and the when of it.'

Ashby and his brood vociferously rowed in behind Blayney, sweeping aside any doubt.

Satisfied by Skeet Blayney's story, the questioner said, 'Ya know, Hal, dunno what poison got into you and John's blood, but I reckon your pa is whirling in his grave right now.'

Several men gathered round Hal to help Spencer march him to jail, jostling to be the one who slammed the cell door on him. A small, crooked-spined man warned Spencer, 'You get Bannion's neck in a noose fast, Speck, or we'll do it for ya.'

This brought a rousing chorus of approval, the robustness of which threatened to splinter the rafters in the jam-packed law office.

'You need have no worries, fellas,' Spencer reassured the baying crowd. 'As Sheriff, you have my word that Hal Bannion is ropebait.'

Charles Ashby summoned Frank Benning, the town council chairman, forward. 'Frank, we've got a new sheriff to swear in!' Then, turning to the crowd, he announced, 'After the swearing-in, the drinks at the Cat's Paw are on me!'

The cheer for this was even louder than the call for Hal's hanging.

'I need a deputy, too,' Speck Spencer demanded.

'This bastard Bannion will need constant watchin'.'

'Seems reasonable to me,' Ashby agreed.

'I reckon it'll be OK,' Benning approved, 'but only until Bannion is strung up. After that there'll be no call for a deputy. The town coffers can't afford one anyway.'

Ashby generously volunteered, 'I'll pay the deputy's salary, and I reckon Skeet Blayney will make a good one.'

No one, except Hal Bannion, was of a mind to challenge the Ashby gunnie's nomination, and he figured he'd be puffing wasted breath if he did. Besides, he had enough on his plate thinking about swinging in the breeze from the great oak at the south end of Main that served as the town gallows.

Spencer's swearing-in over pronto, everyone except Skeet Blayney headed for the Cat's Paw to swig Ashby's free rot-gut. The new sheriff assigned him the first watch, which made Blayney as happy as a eunuch in a cat house. Disgruntled, Blayney took to entertaining himself by telling Hal how slickly Ashby had got his neck in a noose.

'It was all Ashby's idea,' Blayney confirmed, 'having you strung up for Bradley's murder. He reckons he's killed two birds with the one stone. Ashby's got big plans, and he reckoned Bradley would have been a thorn in his side.'

For the next couple of minutes, Hal traded insults with Blayney, working on his temper, until the shyster deputy exploded.

'Any more lip from you, Bannion, and I'll step into that cell and beat you senseless!'

Hal saw his chance and grabbed it. He continued baiting Blayney until his anger peaked. Blayney grabbed the keys and charged the cell door.

'I'm goin' to teach you a lesson that you'll never forget, Bannion,' he snarled.

'You ain't got the guts, Blayney,' Hal taunted. 'Nor the brains neither.'

Blayney lunged wildly at Hal, his ape-like hands intent on throttling him. Bannion, lighter of foot, side-stepped, stuck out a leg and tripped his would-be mauler and, as he toppled forward, spun around to put his boot on Blayney's rump to pitch him headlong into the wall. Hal's stomach heaved at the sound of Skeet Blayney's head impacting on the rough stone. The man folded with a whimper.

Hal tore strips from the bunk sheet, bound Blayney's hands and feet and gagged him. He locked the cell door behind him. Seconds later, he was on the boardwalk, free, but only until he heard the sound of a cocked gun from the shadows.

SIX

'Knew you'd get up to somethin',' Speck Spencer chuckled. 'By the sound of that ruckus, Blayney's goin' to be real sore when he comes to.' He stepped from the shadows to order, 'Back inside, Bannion.'

He ordered Hal to haul Blayney's limp body out of the cell before locking him back in it, then he threw a pitcher of cold water on Blayney's face.

'Some deppity you made,' he growled contemptuously.

Woozily, Blayney got to his feet.

'Tell you what,' Spencer said, 'I'll referee a rematch, but there'll have to be rules now.' He laughed leerily. 'Well, only two rules.' His rattlesnake eyes rested on Hal Bannion. 'You stand and Skeet hits; you move and I shoot.'

An idiot grin lit Skeet Blayney's face. 'Them's real good rules, Speck.'

'Glad you like 'em, Skeet.'

The next five minutes brought a hellish punishment to Hal Bannion's body. Good sense would have him fold, but pride made him stand. Eventually Blayney ran out of steam.

Departing, Spencer advised, 'You'd best get a good night's sleep, Bannion. I like a frisky hangin'.'

The office door opened to reveal Ruth Sullivan, carrying a bottle of Ashby's best whiskey.

'What d'ya want?' Spencer snapped.

'I've come to visit the prisoner, Sheriff.'

'Bannion hates your guts,' Blayney spat. 'He never did like you pleasurin' his brother.'

'Nice of you to bring a bottle, Ruth,' Spencer said, grabbing the bottle from her as she went past.

Ruth tried to grab the bottle back, but Spencer shoved her aside. Then, sniggering. 'I've got to search you, Ruth.'

'Search me?'

'Yeah. You might have a gun in your petticoats, you see.'

'Yeah,' Blayney giggled. 'Want me to hold her fer yeh, Speck?'

Ruth Sullivan went stiff as winter ice as Spencer's hands roamed freely. 'Can't find no gun,' he concluded. 'But then I guess to be certain, I'd best let my deppity check too.'

Skeet Blayney was even bolder than Spencer, and if Charles Ashby and a couple of his cronies had not arrived, Ruth reckoned she would have paid a high price for her visit to Hal Bannion.

'Ruth, honey,' Ashby greeted cordially, and looked to Spencer for an explanation for her presence.

'Came to visit, Bannion,' he said surlily, his fun spoiled.

'Didn't think you two were friends, Ruth?' Ashby said.

'I'm visiting because it's what John Bannion would have wanted.'

'Where are your manners?' the saloon owner rebuked Spencer and Blayney. 'Don't just stand there. See the lady through to the prisoner.'

'My whiskey,' Ruth demanded.

Spencer handed over the bottle grudgingly. Overall, Ruth reckoned the visit was going pretty well; well enough to give her confidence that her next visit would have Hal Bannion out of jail. Going past Spencer, she taunted, 'Tough luck about the bottle, Speck.'

'I'll get even,' he promised in an undertone.

Ruth was counting on it.

Hal Bannion's jaw dropped when he saw Ruth Sullivan. She was the last one in Crosby Flats he'd have expected to come calling. His disapproval of his brother's association with Ruth was no secret.

'Hello, Hal. I hear you've got yourself in something of a pickle.'

'You might say.' Considering Ruth, he let his views be known. 'You know Bannions ain't popular round here, Ruth, and God knows my tongue hasn't been kind to you in the past, so. . . ?'

'John would expect me to call, Hal.'

'I appreciate you dropping by, surely, But I reckon there'll be a price to pay for your kindness.'

'I've been paying a price all my life, Hal. It don't matter none that I'll have to pay now.'

'I thought you were a passenger on today's stage out of town.'

'I was.'

'So, why'd you stay?'

'That don't matter none.'

'I'd like to know, Ruth.'

'Well, I figured that with the mood in this town, with you bucking Ashby, it was likely you'd end up right where you are, or in the funeral parlour. So I decided to stay around to help you, or bury you.'

There was a commotion in the outer office that got their attention, and a second later Alice Bramwell burst anxiously through to the cells, coming up short on seeing Ruth Sullivan, her face showing surprise and no small amount of disappointment.

Spencer came to lean against the cell next to Hal's, a sneer curling his lips. 'You're a real pop'lar fella with the ladies, Bannion. There's goin' to be a barrel of tears shed tomorrow when you're blowin' in the wind.' Departing, he doffed his hat to Alice. 'Miss Bramwell, ma'am. Nice havin' you call.' Then, turning an evil eye on Ruth Sullivan, snorted. 'You still, ah . . . *entertainin'*, Ruth?'

Hal strained through the bars to reach Spencer, but he stepped back a few paces out of his reach. 'You've got a filthy mouth that needs shutting, Spencer,' he growled.

'Well, you ain't goin' to do the shuttin', Bannion. 'Less it's your ghost will.'

Alice, disturbed by Hal's staunch defence of Ruth Sullivan, murmured, 'I guess you've got all the company you need, Hal.'

She fled, ignoring Hal's holler.

'Guess that gal is in love with you, Hal Bannion,' Ruth Sullivan opined.

Bannion dismissed the idea as loco. 'The only Bannion Alice Bramwell had an eye for was John, Ruth.'

'Ain't so. John used to say that Alice trailing his coat tail was her way of staying close to you.'

'Oh, get along with you you, Ruth,' Hal chuckled.

Ruth elaborated. 'Alice thought you weren't keen on her, So, she being all doe-eyed about you, the only way she could get to be around you was to suck up to John.'

Hal chortled. 'What's this, Ruth, comfort for the doomed man?'

'Don't believe it if you want, but that's the way it was.' Ruth shook her head. 'And is. Even a blind man could see that, the way she hared out of here just now.'

'Well, one thing's for sure: you've given me a whole lot of thinking to do, Ruth.' Hal's spirits slumped. 'If what you say is true, it sure is a shame I won't be around to check out its veracity.'

Ruth smiled. 'Oh, I don't know about that.'

'It would take the Lord himself to get me out of this one,' Hal sighed.

'Or a Chinaman.'

Hal was left to puzzle over Ruth Sullivan's departing statement and, ponder as he might, he could not unravel its meaning.

SEVEN

Ruth Sullivan marched straight down Main towards the hotel for as long as Speck Spencer's eyes were on her, but as soon as he withdrew into the law office, she cut an angle across Main into the shadows of an alley that led to the side door of Yang's Laundry. She gave a pre-arranged coded knock on the door. Being Chinese, Yang lived under constant threat, some folk not wanting him around. Night callers, unless he was summoned from the room behind the laundry by the secret knock that he'd given Ruth Sullivan, he never answered.

Yang's yellow moon face appeared at the glass-panelled door, lit ghostly by a coal-oil lamp. On seeing Ruth, he beamed a smile and opened the door to usher her quickly inside, and then leaned out the door to check the alley for unwelcome callers.

'Me think you gone, 'Uth.' Yang couldn't pronounce an R if his life depended on it.

'I've got one or two things to do first, Yang.'

'You want yellow powder?'

'Yes.'

'Me get.'

Yang hurried through to the back room and returned, seconds later, with a small packet of the yellow powder that he'd been supplying to Ruth for over a year. Yang had explained to her that it came from some roots, but had a name that Yang did not know the English for and Ruth couldn't understand the Chinese name of, so, it became the yellow powder.

Yang's face was puzzled. 'If you not woman who lie with men, why you want yellow powder, 'Uth?'

'One last little chore to perform, Yang.'

Yang's fingers closed over Ruth Sullivan's dollars. 'You good woman, 'Uth.'

After checking the alley, he let her out and quickly closed the door. Ruth heard a bolt slide home, and then a second. She couldn't understand why Yang stayed in Crosby Flats to live in nightly fear from any liquored-up no-good who wanted to vent his spleen on someone whom no one, with the exception of Ed Bradley, would lift a finger to help. The late sheriff had given Yang a fair shake but, with him dead, Yang would be in even greater peril.

Ruth paused at the opening from the alley to

look along Main and the streets off it. Finding them deserted, she hurried across the street and kept up her fleet-footed pace to the hotel. On reaching her room, she carefully deposited the yellow powder in a drawer and went to bed smiling.

Hal Bannion laid back on his bunk and looked through his cell window at the lover's moon drifting across a cloudless sky. His thoughts were jumbled by the two women in his mind. He was acutely aware, and even more acutely ashamed, of how wrong he'd been about Ruth Sullivan.

'Ruth's a fine woman, Hal, if you give her the chance to be.' John Bannion's words of praise echoed back to Hal. 'Better than most in these parts. For two pins I'd marry her.'

The idea of John tying the knot with Ruth Sullivan had given Hal a thousand restless nights, but now he was coming round to thinking that his brother could have done a whole lot worse than make Ruth Sullivan his wife.

More words came back to Hal, Ruth Sullivan's.

'Guess that gal is in love with you, Hal Bannion.'

Hal let his mind drift back over Alice Bramwell's visits to the Broken Spur, and he couldn't find a single shred of evidence that would give credence to Ruth Sullivan's assertion that Alice Bramwell was in love with him, and not John.

'Don't matter much anyway,' he mumbled soul-fully, 'if you can't keep your head out of a noose.'

Rack his brains as he might, he could not find a way out of his predicament. There was no way that Skeet Blayney, who had been handed the night watch by Spencer, would fall for his ruse, again.

He went to the window and peered out at the oak that he'd probably he swinging from on the morrow. It cast a long shadow, as if reaching for him. He sighed a sigh as lingering as his last breath would be.

EIGHT

Skeet Blayney delivered his breakfast at 7 a.m. 'Sure is a shame to waste a breakfast on you, Bannion.'

Hal ate the meal to spite Blayney, whose eyes followed every mouthful down his throat. He did not get to finish his meal, Speck Spencer came to haul him off to the makeshift court in the Cat's Paw Saloon. Crosby Flats had not risen to having a proper courthouse, and neither a proper judge. That function was performed by Barnabas Leary, a ne'er-do-well who had spent a couple of years in a Boston law school, before his fondness for whiskey overtook his zeal for the law. He now acted as Crosby Flats' judge, preacher and undertaker.

'Back off,' Spencer ordered the crowd jamming the street in front of the jail, as he shoved Hal through the blood-thirsty mob. Spencer's concern was not for Hal Bannion, he'd gladly throw him to the crowd and be done with it, but Ashby wanted the pretence of justice to be upheld, and what Ashby wanted, Ashby got.

'Murdering bastard. . . .'

'Don't waste a trial. . . .'

'Run him straight to the hanging tree. . . .'

'In a little while,' Spencer said. He picked out one of the mob. 'Get a rope over a branch of that oak, Bart.'

Skeet Blayney sniggered. 'I guess folk would rather have a rattlesnake in their house than a Bannion.'

Hal was jostled every step of the way to the Cat's Paw. When he entered the makeshift courtroom, he glanced at the line of unopened whiskey bottles on the bar, and knew the verdict was already in. He was, as Speck Spencer said the night before: ropebait!

Spencer flung Hal into a chair and he and Blayney stood either side of him. Hal reckoned they'd like nothing better than for him to try and break out, which would give them the opportunity to use the guns they had been so anxious to use the day before, when Alice Bramwell spoked their wheels.

Ashby, gently, if annoyedly, pulled Barnabas Leary upright in his chair behind a long table on the stage and rapped his gavel for him.

'Dearly beloved brethren, we are gathered here today . . .' Leary began.

Ashby dug his elbow in Leary's ribs. 'Wrong speech, Judge,' he laughed.

'Maybe not,' one of the saloon doves called out. 'After all this is as near to a funeral as makes no diff'rence.'

The bar room exploded in laughter. There was even a shadow of a smile on Hal Bannion's lips.

Ashby reminded Leary, 'Barnabas, you're a judge now, you can be undertaker and preacher later.'

Leary, his watery eyes already glazed, dived under the table to sup from a pocket flask. When he came back up he had his wits restored and, clearing his throat, authoritatively ordered Spencer, 'Present the accused and your evidence, Sheriff, ah. . . .'

'Spencer,' Ashby supplied.

'Right,' Leary slurred. 'Sheriff Spike.'

'Stand up, Bannion,' Spencer growled. 'This is Hal Bannion, Ed Bradley's murderer.'

'Hold on there, Sheriff ah. . . .'

'Spencer,' Ashby again supplied.

'Spiller,' Leary boomed out. 'I can't just take your word on this man Spencer's guilt.'

'I'm Spencer, you old fool,' the new sheriff blasted. His finger stabbed at Hal. 'Bannion's his name.'

Barnabas Leary coughed. 'Bundle, yes.'

Ashby rapped Leary's gavel, commanding silence in a saloon that was in uproar.

'The judge is right, Speck,' he rebuked Spencer. 'Tell His Honour your reasons for believing Hal Bannion's guilty of murder.'

'Damn it!' The jury foreman shot out of his chair. 'Bannion was caught red-handed. What more evidence is needed? And he threatened Sheriff Bradley too, when he had that skirmish with you last night, Mr Ashby. I heard him m'self. So, let's get a rope and have justice done for our late Sheriff.'

A chorus of approval for the foreman's bluntness rang out.

'What chance have I got of a fair trial, if the foreman of the jury has already made up his mind, Your Honour?' Hal protested.

'This will be a fair trial,' Barnabas Leary pronounced. 'You have my word on that Mr, ah . . . Bundle.' Leary's reassurance lasted all of ten seconds before Ashby's evil-eyed glare had the judge back-peddling.

'Of course, it does look like you did kill Sheriff ah . . . Bumbley.'

Barnabas Leary dived under the table again to slug from his flask. The hilarity in the Cat's Paw reached a new peak. Speck Spencer and Skeet Blayney told their lies, and it took only seconds for the jury to put their heads together and come up with a guilty verdict.

Spencer and Blayney grabbed Hal and were frog-marching him out of the saloon when Ashby intervened, playing the role of honest broker right to the end.

'Hold on now, fellas. Another day won't make a difference. It's only right and proper that Bannion be given the chance to make things right with his Maker, and be given the opportunity to appeal the court's verdict, if he so wishes.'

Some murmured in favour of Ashby's stand; others, their hanging lust thwarted, glared angrily. There were no objectors though. Every man there knew that it was a mighty unhealthy thing to disagree with the saloon owner.

'A mighty fine and noble gesture, sir,' Barnabas Leary loftily intoned, in his one moment of lucid thought since the charade began.

Ashby, as sly as a fox in a henhouse, placated the crowd. 'No need to stop the celebrations though now that, in my opinion, we've had justice done.'

Barnabas Leary led the charge to the bar. Charles Ashby strolled to where Spencer and Blayney held Hal Bannion.

'I guess you fellas had better take the prisoner back to jail,' he sneered. 'You should have just ridden out when you had the chance, Bannion.'

'I don't know how it's going to happen, Ashby,' Hal promised, 'but I'm going to get even with you.'

Ashby's sneer deepened. 'I'm not afraid of ghosts, Bannion.'

'C'mon,' Spencer growled, and shoved Bannion

ahead of him, 'I've got this awful thirst I want to slake.'

'Me, too, Speck,' Blayney whined. 'I ain't goin' to be stuck in that jail all day, am I?'

'You're my deppity, and you'll do as you're told,' Spencer flung back.

Ruth Sullivan came up to Bannion. 'Hello, Hal. Sorry.'

'Thanks, Ruth,' Bannion smiled. ' 'Preciate your neighbourliness.'

'I'll call to see you later.'

'I'll look forward to your visit, Ruth.'

'I'll bring a bottle, too.'

Hal was at a loss to understand Ruth's fondness for bringing him liquor, he being a man who limited his drinking to special occasions.

'You do that, Ruth,' Spencer laughed.

'You ain't going to grab it, are you, Speck?' Ruth asked fearfully.

His and Blayney's laughter went up a notch. Spencer feigned shock.

'Ruth, how could you say such a thing? I'm a lawman. Sworn to protect the citizens.'

'And their bottles, too,' Skeet Blayney guffawed.

'See you later,' Ruth told Hal.

'Are you the law 'round here?' the stranger, who had just ridden in, enquired of Spencer, who was dragging Hal back to the jail.

'Who's asking?' Spencer's glance went to the blanket-draped body tied to the piebald the hatchet-jawed man had in tow.

'The name's, Bascombe.'

'Jess Bascombe, the bounty hunter?' Skeet Blayney quizzed in awe.

'The same,' Bascombe answered dead-eyed. His head jerked to the piebald. 'That's Jack Scrapp, and he's worth five hundred dollars. I'm here to collect.'

Spencer said, 'I don't know if we've got that much in the kitty, Bascombe.'

Charles Ashby had strolled on to the saloon porch, Bascombe having piqued his interest. He was thinking that a man of Jess Bascombe's killing instincts might be of service to him.

'I'll cover if there's not enough in the town, Sheriff,' he promised.

Bascombe let his gaze drift Ashby's way. 'A mighty fine gesture, sir.'

Ruth Sullivan returned to the hotel. On reaching her room, she went to the drawer and took out the packet of yellow powder that she had been given by Yang the night before. Her smile was one of pure mischief. She took a bottle of whiskey from the same drawer and added the yellow powder to it, then shook the bottle until the powder dissolved completely. She put the cork back on the bottle, and put the bottle back in the drawer. She chuckled. 'Should be just about right come dark, I reckon.'

NINE

For Hal Bannion, it was a long day. Skeet Blayney's humour soured by the minute as Spencer failed to put in an appearance and, when he did, it was to crash flat on his face on the floor. Blayney kicked his unconscious body hard.

Bannion had worked relentlessly on Blayney's humour in the hope of riling him enough to make him careless, but the Ashby hardcase had learned his lesson well and did not rise to Hal's baiting.

Throughout the day, Ruth Sullivan had kept a constant watch on proceedings and, at dusk, on seeing Speck Spencer stagger towards the law office, she reckoned the time was ripe to start her plan of action for Hal Bannion's escape.

She hid the bottle of doctored whiskey under her coat, not risking some liquored-up no-good grabbing it from her. On leaving the hotel, Ruth made straight for the jail, carrying the bait that she was certain Skeet Blayney would be unable to resist. She was right. As soon as she put her foot across the threshold of the law-office, Skeet Blayney grabbed the bottle of whiskey and slugged deeply from it. Wiping his mouth with the back of his hand, his eyes took in Ruth Sullivan's form, his evil thoughts glinting in his dirty-water eyes.

Ruth was not worried. A couple of minutes from now, Skeet Blayney would not be able to raise a finger.

Hal was puzzled by Ruth's jaunty humour. 'Won't be long now, Hal.' Half a minute later, Skeet Blayney crashed to the floor. Ruth hurried back outside to the office and returned with the key. Bannion leaped through the cell door and kissed Ruth.

'Why, Hal Bannion,' she chided mirthfully. 'What has gotten into you?' She shoved him ahead of her. 'Go on. Get out of here.'

'You're coming too, Ruth.'

'Me?'

'You can't stay. With the mood around here, helping a Bannion might make them use the noose on you that was planned for me.' Hal studied Ruth. 'I never thought I'd hear myself say this, Ruth: you're a fine woman, and John could have done a whole lot worse than taking you for his wife.'

'Kind of you to say so, Hal.' Ruth smiled

ruefully. 'If a little late, I might add.' She shoved him ahead of her. 'Now, will you get out of here while you still can?'

Hal collected his sixgun and a rifle on his way out.

'Where will you go?' Ruth asked.

'Ain't sure. Anywhere away from Crosby Flats will be good.'

'Hal. . . .'

Bannion pulled up. 'Yeah?'

'About John's gambling spree, and this preacher. . . .'

Curiosity spiked, Hal coaxed, 'I'm listening, Ruth.'

'Well, thing is, this preacher man didn't know his Bible.' Ruth's, face creased in thought. 'My Uncle Willy was a preacher and my daddy was as good as, so I grew up on Bible readings.' She scowled. 'Morning, noon and night Bible readings until I was blue in the face. So I'd know a preacher when I heard one, and the Reverend Goodwood was no preacher, Hal.' Ruth shrugged. 'I don't know what good knowing's going to do.'

'Go on, Ruth. There's more, ain't there?'

Ruth frowned. 'I figure that the preacher was Charles Ashby's agent in that poker game that John got sucked into.'

'We're of the one mind on that, Ruth. Did this Goodwood say where he was headed?'

'I heard Ashby mention a place on the border

called San Julio, or something like that.'

'Thanks, Ruth.'

Hal hugged her, and then hurried along Main, door dodging to the livery. He had one or two close calls as men stopped, their drunken eyes catching a glimpse of him, but, luckily, no one interested enough to investigate further than a preliminary glance, none believing that he was seeing right, Hal supposed.

Hal reached the livery. He paused just outside the circle of yellow light from a storm lantern hanging above the entrance. It was an ever-changing circle: the lantern's light stirred by the wind dipped and flourished, causing the circle to narrow and widen. He hugged the ragged edge of the circle and had a few tense seconds as the wind died and the lantern flared brilliantly, putting him in plain sight. It left him with no choice but to abandon his cautious approach. For once luck favoured him. He heard loud snoring from the loft and, through a gap in the floor-boards, spotted the livery hand out cold, an empty whiskey bottle at his feet. Able to move freely, Hal saddled his horse quickly and was riding into the darkness when a man near the Cat's Paw Saloon shouted:

'Hey, ain't that Hal Bannion I'm seein'?'

Several guns opened up at once. Bullets buzzed around Bannion. Chunks of wood, each one as deadly as a bullet, were ripped from the livery wall. He wheeled his horse about, but more guns spat to cut off his retreat.

He was a sitting target in the storm lantern's light!

Hal swept his rifle from its saddle scabbard and sent a round into the lantern. It crashed to the ground in a fiery ball that spooked his horse. Unsettled in the saddle, he was thrown as the horse reared. Ignoring his pain, he corkscrewed into a crouch and rattled off bullets as fast as he could. The men scattered, but by now, led by Charles Ashby, more men were spilling from the Cat's Paw. The sixguns were quickly replaced by rifles, and the risk to Hal's hide soared.

'Don't let him get away!' Ashby ordered.

A row of jostling shooters lined up, every man anxious to curry favour with Ashby. Hal counted down the last seconds of his life.

TEN

Ruth Sullivan, her heart near stilled, watched from the law-office window. There was no way that Hal Bannion could survive the guns lining up against him. She was the only hope he had. She had no choice but to declare in his favour.

Ruth grabbed a shotgun from the gun rack and scampered outside, hoping that the jostling for position to be Bannion's executioner would give her the precious seconds she needed. On reaching the boardwalk, Ruth did not hesitate. The shotgun blast ripped a jagged hole in the porch overhang of the Cat's Paw, debris spewed out all around forcing the shooters to scatter, some howling as flying fragments found a mark. She hoped the ensuing confusion would hand Hal the chance to escape.

'I'll cut in half the first man that moves!' Ruth warned, and called to Bannion, 'Hit the trail, Hal!'

'Not without you, Ruth,' he yelled back.

Bannion vaulted into the saddle and, keeping low, made a headlong dash for the law-office.

'Are you crazy?' Ruth said, but her smile was the kind a cat has after cream.

Hal grabbed the shotgun and unleashed the second load. Flinging the weapon aside, he reached down to hoist Ruth aboard the horse and charged out of town, his departure dogged by flashing guns.

'Keep low, Ruth,' Hal advised. 'Make yourself as small a target as you can.'

After one thunderous clatter of guns, Ruth's encircling arms jerked and went slack. Alarmed, Hal glanced over his shoulder and the blood drained to his toes.

Breathlessly, Ruth said, 'Keep going, Hal. I'll be fine.'

'Mount up,' Ashby shouted. 'Don't let that murderer and his trash get away.'

The men scrambled for their horses, most of them discovering that liquored senses and horse riding don't jell. The half sober ones, fired up by Ashby's promise, 'Two hundred a man when Bannion swings, or on delivery of his corpse', formed an ad hoc posse that thundered off after Bannion, fast closing the gap that had opened up.

Bannion, forced to pick up the pace, felt Ruth's hold on him slip further, and he had to reach back to keep her in the saddle.

'Save yourself, Hal,' Ruth breathed, her eyes wild with pain.

'We're going to make it out of here together, Ruth,' he vowed. He switched direction towards the Big B, not liking the idea of having to ask for Luther Bramwell's help. Being beholden to Bramwell went against the Bannion grain, and he might not give Ruth sanctuary anyway, but he had no option but to seek the man's help, because by now Ruth was mumbling incoherently and in danger of tumbling from the saddle.

He ducked into a dark hollow and took a calculated risk on Ashby's posse riding past. His gamble paid off and, as soon as their dust settled, Hal made tracks as fast as he could for the Big B.

ELEVEN

Luther Bramwell was annoyed at Alice's out of tune singing and discordant piano playing. The Bramwells' guest was an up-and-coming politician and banker, whom most folk tipped to be governor one day, and in the not too distant future. Luther and Mary Bramwell considered John Newton to be ideal husband material.

'Sorry,' Alice apologized. 'I fear my mind just isn't on singing tonight.'

'You sang like an angel, Alice, my dear,' Newton complimented.

'Then you must be tone deaf, Mr Newton, sir,' Alice replied rebelliously. She had become increasingly tired of being trotted out like a prize filly to a procession of prospective husbands.

'Alice!' Mary Bramwell rebuked. 'You will apologize to Mr Newton immediately, I don't know what's got into you.'

Alice sprang off the piano stool. 'You know very well what's got into me, Mother,' she flared. 'The man I love will be hanged tomorrow morning, and' – her blue eyes, lit by a fire of derision locked with her father's – 'plead as I might, you will not lift a finger to help him.'

'Enough of this nonsense, Alice!' Luther Bramwell bellowed. 'Hal Bannion is a convicted murderer. There is nothing to be done.'

'Hal wouldn't swat a fly!'

Mary Bramwell stamped her feet and commanded Alice, 'Stop this nonsense at once. Mr Newton is our guest, and does not deserve your graceless behaviour. You must make it up to him.'

Alice Bramwell's defiant glare took in both her parents. 'Will you, for heaven's sake, stop trying to marry me off to every man who happens along?'

'Really,' Mary Bramwell wailed, seeking her husband's support as she tottered in shock.

Alice was not finished. 'You both know that I've loved Hal Bannion all my life, and it's he alone I want to marry.'

John Newton, his pride crushed, stood stiffly. 'My compliments, ma'am, sir. I think it best I should leave now.'

Mary Bramwell fretted. 'Another glass of wine surely, Mr Newton?'

'I think not, ma'am.'

As Newton marched out of the room, Mary Bramwell wailed, 'Do something, Luther.'

The rancher was at a loss as to know what to do.

'Good night, Miss Bramwell,' Newton said huffily as he went by.

'Good night, sir. A safe journey to you.'

Mary Bramwell stood in shock. 'She's going to be an old maid, Luther,' she swooned. Bramwell caught her as she slumped to the floor.

'Pour your mother a brandy,' Luther Bramwell ordered Alice, and as Mary Bramwell drifted hazily back to consciousness, he told his daughter, 'We have a lot to talk about, young lady.' He glowered. If you deserve that appendage after what's happened?'

'I'm sorry, Father, but how can I care about anything with Hal Bannion facing a noose tomorrow? My life is over.'

'Hal Bannion is a murderer and penniless,' Bramwell raged.

'You seem unsure as to which is the greater sin,' Alice chanted.

'And even if he weren't either,' Luther Bramwell thundered, 'there would still be no place in this house for a Bannion.'

'Aren't you ever going to forgive him for not selling you the Broken Spur? Why should he? Hal had every bit as much right to ranch as you have.'

'Cows need grass, Alice,' her father raged on, 'and I aim to get every blade there is in this valley and beyond. The Spur was going down the pipe anyway.

I've already spoken to Charles Ashby about buying the Bannion place, and he isn't opposed to the idea, him not being a ranching man and' – his eyes slid away from his daughter's – 'wifeless.'

Alice became breathless with alarm. 'You wouldn't. . . ? You couldn't. . . ? *I won't!*'

'Oh, I'll admit that Ashby wouldn't be my first choice,' Bramwell growled, 'but with you shunning every suitor your mother and I come up with . . . and he's got to be better than a damn Bannion!'

'You can't buy the Broken Spur. John Bannion was cheated by Ashby. That makes the Spur stolen property.'

'John Bannion lost fair and square, Alice.'

'When did Ashby ever run a fair game?'

'It isn't my affair,' Bramwell stated bluntly. 'John Bannion was a grown man. He knew what he was doing.'

'If you buy the Broken Spur from Ashby, I'll never speak another word to you, Father.'

'Oh, what's got into to her, Luther?' Mary Bramwell wailed.

'Don't you go fainting again,' Luther warned his wife crossly.

Mary Bramwell began to weep piteously.

'On the other hand,' Luther mumbled. 'And where do you think you're going, young lady?' he enquired, as Alice fled the room.

'To help Hal Bannion. As I should have long before now.'

'How, may I ask?'

'I don't know, yet. I'll find a way, even if it means marching right into the sheriff's office. With a cocked gun.'

Alice was dressing for the journey to town when she heard the sound of an approaching rider. She raced to the front door to peer into the pitch darkness. 'Who is it? Who's there?' Her heart leaped on seeing Hal Bannion coming out of the night. She ran to him, wild with relief. 'They let you go, Hal? I prayed for a miracle and it hap—' Alice came up short when she saw Ruth Sullivan, and asked sourly, 'What's she doing here? Why is she with you, Hal?'

'Ruth's caught a bullet, Alice. I need help.'

'What the devil's going on?' Luther Bramwell had come to the front door. 'You.' He glared at Hal.

Bannion swung a leg over his saddle horn and dropped to the ground, and took Ruth in his arms to help her down. 'I know you hate Bannion guts, Bramwell. I'm not asking mercy for myself. Ruth's been shot. She needs a doctor and nursing.'

'You can't allow that *creature* in the house, Luther,' Mary Bramwell ranted.

'I've got nowhere else to go, Bramwell,' Hal stated flatly. 'I know we've had our differences, but I believe that you're a Christian man, who won't refuse help to a wounded soul.'

'Luther, if you—'

'Ah, shush, woman,' Bramwell rebuked his wife.

'I wouldn't turn away a wounded dog. Bring her inside, Bannion.'

'I'm beholden, sir,' Hal thanked the rancher.

'Alice. Mary. You help get Ruth settled. I'll saddle up and ride to town to fetch Doc Simmons.'

Alice helped Hal get Ruth Sullivan inside the house, and Mary Bramwell, moved by the sight of the maimed woman, overcame her objections to her presence and hurried ahead to prepare a bed for Ruth as Hal took her upstairs in his arms.

Settled down, Ruth grabbed hold of Hal's hand and urged him, 'Ride out, Hal, while you can. It won't take long for Ashby's brood to figure out that if you didn't vanish into thin air, you must have headed here.'

'I'm staying put, Ruth,' Hal said grimly.

'No you're not,' Alice Bramwell intervened. 'Ruth is right. If Ashby's riders find you here, they'll hang you, of that you can be sure.'

'Listen to Alice,' Ruth urged Hal. Her smile was weak, but warm. 'A man should listen to his future wife.' Alice blushed to the roots of her hair. 'And you've got unfinished business to take care of in San Julio.'

'It can wait. I'll get around to the Reverend Goodwood soon enough.'

Ruth's anger flared to leave her limp and breathless. 'You owe it to John to get back the ranch that Ashby cheated him out of, and to do that you'll have to find Goodwood and make him talk.'

'But. . . .'

'I'll be fine, Hal. I'm sure Alice and Mrs Bramwell will take good care of me.'

'We surely will,' Mary Bramwell testified.

'I'll be back, Ruth,' he promised.

'And I'll be right here.'

'You'll need a fresh horse,' Alice Bramwell said.

Hal quickly followed Alice to the stables.

'What happened back in town, Hal? How did you and Ruth Sullivan get tied up?'

'Ruth busted me out of jail, Alice. Then, when it looked like I was going to my Maker, Ruth stepped in again. I couldn't leave her in town to face Ashby and his cronies. When we were riding out, Ruth caught a bullet.'

'Looks like Ruth Sullivan thinks a great deal of you, Hal.'

'She did what she did, because she figured it would be what John wanted her to do, but I've got to admit, Alice, that I truly was unjust in my utterances against Ruth. John might be alive today, if I hadn't spoken out so loudly against him marrying her.'

On reaching the stables, Alice said, 'Take Midnight. No horse in these parts will keep up with him.'

'You're a fine woman, Alice,' Hal said. 'And one day you'll make a man a fine wife, too.' Hal slung a saddle on the stallion and vaulted into it.

'Good luck, Hal.'

'Do your best for Ruth,' he asked of her.

'I will,' she promised.

On impulse Hal reached down and, encircling her waist, lifted her clear off the ground to kiss her. 'Don't know whether I've done right or wrong, Alice,' he said, 'but I reckon I should have done that a long time ago.'

'God bless and keep you, Hal Bannion,' she murmured as he galloped into the night, only seconds before the makeshift posse thundered into the yard.

Ed Lacy, an Ashby hanger-on, drew rein, stirring a cloud of choking dust. 'Miss Bramwell, ma'am. Has that murderer Bannion and Ruth Sullivan been this way?'

'Ruth is in the house. Hal is long gone.'

Lacy delegated two men. 'You fellas haul Ruth Sullivan back to town. The rest of us will dog Bannion's tail.'

Alice Bramwell hurried ahead to the house and took a rifle from the gun cabinet in Luther Bramwell's study. She was back in the hall as the men whom Lacy had delegated to get Ruth stepped through the front door.

'Ruth stays right where she is,' Alice said. 'Take another step and you fellas are dead.'

The men beckoned to Lacy and, when he joined them, he warned Alice, 'You're impeding a posse, ma'am, and giving sanctuary to a law-breaker.'

'You're not a posse, Ed Lacy,' Alice scoffed,

'you're Ashby's scum. You can haul me off to jail if you want to, but Ruth Sullivan is wounded and she stays put until she's well enough to make her own decision on whether to go or stay.'

One of the two delegated men stepped forward. 'Me for one ain't takin' no lip from a woman.' He leaped back as a bullet from Alice's rifle buzzed the toecap of his right boot. She restated grimly, 'Like I said, Ruth Sullivan stays put.'

Hal Bannion had doubled back to watch from the tall spruce trees to the south of the barn, fearing trouble for the Bramwell women, with Luther off to town. 'Needn't have worried,' he smiled, as he saw Lacy and his cohorts back out of the house under the threat of Alice Bramwell's Winchester. He had been in love with Alice Bramwell before, but now that love deepened greatly.

He turned and took Midnight quietly up through the trees. On reaching the crest of the hill overlooking the house, he gave the stallion his head for Mexico.

TWELVE

Charles Ashby stomped about his office behind the Cat's Paw Saloon, trying to find words that were vitriolic enough to voice his thoughts about the posse's withdrawal from the Bramwell place, their tails between their legs.

'I figured you'd not want any trouble with Luther Bramwell, Mr Ashby,' Ed Lacy whined in his defence. 'Don't make no sense to me for a man to get Bramwell on his back by bustin' into his house and haulin' off who Alice and Mary Bramwell said was their guest.'

'Guest!' Ashby exploded. 'Ruth Sullivan helped to free a murderer. That makes her a criminal, just like Hal Bannion.'

'You want we should go back out there and haul Ruth in right now?' one of the posse enquired, upstaging Lacy to ingratiate himself with Ashby. 'I'm ready to ride, Mr Ashby.'

Ashby looked with contempt at Lacy. 'You're a good man, Hayes,' he complimented the volunteer. 'But I guess we're going to have to bide our time on this one.'

'Well, any time you want, Mr Ashby, sir. I'm ready,' Hayes said.

Hayes' boot-licking earned Lacy's malevolent scowl.

Ashby flung himself into the chair behind an expansive mahogany desk, befitting, in his opinion, a man of his standing. 'Get out,' he ordered the men who had formed the posse. 'I need to think.'

Five minutes later he was on his way to the jail, where Speck Spencer and Skeet Blayney had slept through the entire shindig of Bannion's break-out and escape. He kicked Spencer hard in the butt to wake him. He came to, groggily rubbing his head. Ashby repeated his treatment of Spencer on Skeet Blayney. Spencer, first to gain his senses, leaped from his bunk on seeing the empty cell where Hal Bannion should be.

'A fine pair of lawmen you are,' Ashby snarled.

'Did they hang Bannion a'ready?' Blayney asked, trying to focus his eyes to determine what part of the day he was in.

'Bannion's gone,' Ashby informed the brain-scrambled duo. 'But you wouldn't know anything about that, would you?'

Skeet Blayney, puzzled, grumbled, 'I only took

one slug o' that bottle that Ruth Sullivan brought Bannion.'

'No doubt laced with that yellow powder she gets from Yang to subdue over-zealous clients. It would knock the kick out of a mule.'

Blayney growled. 'Powder? What damn powder?'

'It was a well-kept secret. I got to know about it when Ruth worked for me at the Cat's Paw.'

'Well, if'n you hadn't kept it a secret...' Blayney grumbled.

Ashby angrily paced the law office. 'Lessons need to be taught and learned in this town, and I figure Yang should be the first to learn that it isn't sensible to buck Charles Ashby.'

'What kinda lesson?' Spencer asked.

Ashby told them.

Hal Bannion kept up a steady but careful pace for over an hour, putting distance between him and the Big B, constantly checking his back-trail as best he could for any sign of pursuit. Satisfied that there was none, he rested the stallion and himself in a shaded creek, surrounded by bush and bramble with a twig strewn ground that would warn him of any nocturnal visitors, two- or four-legged, either of which could prove lethal.

The night was cold and got colder still as the sweat on Hal chilled. His hurried departure left him ill-equipped for sleeping under the stars and, as the night wore on towards dawn, his muscles began to cramp, making sleep impossible. He saddled up at first light, and set a weary course for the Rio Grande, belly rumbling with hunger. He would have to find feed for the stallion. He could hold out, but the horse needed a full belly to give him the energy to outrun any pursuers. Hal was sure there would be followers: Ashby would see to that. With him free and digging, the saloon owner could not take a chance on the dirt that he might produce.

Bannion thought about Jess Bascombe, the bounty hunter. Ashby might very well engage the services of the manhunter to hunt him down. And in Bascombe, Hal reckoned, he'd be hiring a man without scruples. He figured that for the right price, Bascombe would do Ashby's bidding.

Speck Spencer and Skeet Blayney hugged the wall of the alley outside the side door of Yang's laundry. It was dead of night, but they were still careful to hide their presence, because the task that Ashby had handed them needed stealth for a successful conclusion. The Chinaman always slept with an ear open, and could hear a cat purr.

Blayney tiptoed up to the laundry's door and poured the can of kerosene he carried over the door and then along the clapboard walls of the building.

'Give it a few minutes to soak in,' Speck told

Blayney in a whispered instruction. Then, sniggering, 'It should be some bonfire, Skeet.'

Five minutes later, Blayney struck a match, and the instant he touched it to the clapboard structure flame gushed back at him, forcing him to leap back. The fire curled along the walls of the building and raced upwards, filling the alley with an orange light that had Spencer and Blayney scurrying for the dark of the town's backlots to make their way back to the law office. As planned, once the building was well alight they'd raise the alarm and lead Yang's rescue.

The Chinaman sprang up in bed. The crackle of dry timber burning brought a wild fear to his eyes. He looked at the smoke curling in around the edges of the door, and puffing in larger measure under the ill-fitting structure. Squealing in alarm, Yang ran to the door and yanked it open. His eyes filled with an even greater fear on seeing the wall of fire eating its way greedily along the hall, cutting off his escape. The building groaned as the fire ate relentlesly into it. In despair he slammed the door shut and looked desperately around the windowless storeroom that he'd been using as a bedroom since the last attack on him.

He was trapped.

Spencer and Blayney skulked in the law office until the glow of the burning laundry was lighting Main with its fiery orange glow before ringing the fire bell outside the office, one of several placed at strategic locations around town.

'Fire!' Spencer ran into the street, while Blayney sped along Main rattling doors and raising a hullabaloo. Men appeared in nightshirts, some pulling up trousers, but all heading towards Yang's Laundry to help quench the flames, filling buckets from the horse troughs along Main. Spencer and Blayney led the men to Yang's rescue, knowing full well that the Chinaman was already roasted meat.

The flames beat them back to the mouth of the alley and right on to Main as the building crumbled in a fiery inferno, sending clouds of sparks into the air that engaged the rescuers' full attention in quenching, to avoid fire taking hold of several other buildings. Within fifteen minutes, Yang's Laundry was a smouldering, blackened mass of rubble. Charles Ashby sidled up to Spencer and Blayney to congratulate them.

'Nice work, boys.'

Doc Simmons brought news of the fire to the Bramwell Ranch early next morning when he visited Ruth Sullivan. He had spent most of the night trying to patch up her back wound, but none too successfully. She was much too weak to remove the bullet lodged near her spine, and Simmons wasn't sure he was a skilled enough surgeon to try. The operation would almost certainly cause heavy bleeding, and with Ruth as weak as she was he dared not take the risk. Already in the grip of fever from her wound, time was not on Ruth Sullivan's side.

Surfacing from a breathless doze, Ruth struggled to sit up in bed.

'Easy now,' Alice Bramwell advised, settling her back on the pillow.

'Yang's Laundry?' Ruth whispered hoarsely.

Simmons had been relaying the story of the fire to Luther Bramwell as he entered Ruth's bedroom.

'You mustn't upset yourself, Ruth,' Luther Bramwell cautioned.

Alice Bramwell soothed Ruth's brow with a cold cloth.

'My f-fault,' Ruth stammered. 'The f-f-fire.'

'Delirious,' Luther Bramwell concluded.

'Fever as intense as Ruth's can play all sorts of tricks on the mind,' Simmons explained.

'Powd—' Ruth whispered, 'yell-ow powd—' Her eyes closed wearily and she slipped back into a fitful sleep.

Alice helped Doc Simmons dress Ruth's wound.

'It looks really ugly,' Alice observed.

Shaking his head despairingly, Simmons confirmed, 'It is.'

In the hall, Alice asked Simmons bluntly, 'Will Ruth die?'

He shrugged. 'She's lost a lot of blood. Fever has set in. She's very weak.' He rolled his eyes upwards. 'I guess the decision rests elsewhere, Alice.' Getting into his buggy, he said, 'I'll drop by later, but there isn't much I can really do.'

Alice went to sit with Ruth.

Jess Bascombe's hand slipped under his pillow, and his fingers curled around the Peacemaker he always slept with. 'It's open,' he called, in answer to the knock on his hotel room door. As Charles Ashby entered, he relaxed. Men like Ashby were not killers: they sent others to do their dirty work.

Ashby came straight to the point, the way Bascombe liked a man to do.

'Mr Bascombe. I need your services to hunt down a killer.'

'This killer got a name?'

'Yes. Hal Bannion.'

THIRTEEN

If he had a choice, Hal would have given the farm a wide berth, but the stallion needed feed and water, and so did he. He let the horse pick his own way down from the rocky crest overlooking the farmyard. The farmer was the careful kind, probably having had too many unwelcome callers in his time. He pretended not to see Bannion, but Hal had not missed the surreptitious shift of the sod-buster's eyes his way.

The farmer casually rubbed and stretched his back and strolled towards the house. By the time Bannion reached the yard, the farmer was back on the porch with a rifle levelled at him.

'That's far enough, mister, without stating your business.'

'I ain't aiming to bring you grief, sir,' Hal said.

'State your business,' the farmer returned uncompromisingly.

'Food and water for me and my horse.'

The farmer's eyes scanned the terrain behind Hal and, satisfied that he was alone, dropped the rifle's barrel a touch, but not much.

'Where're you headed, stranger?'

'Mexico.'

The rifle barrel came back up. The farmer had seen many men headed for the Rio Grande in his ten years of sod-busting, and most were no-goods. He particularly remembered one, a man with a boy's face and a devil's soul who took his wife from him. Two years later, he found her whoring in a cantina, poxed and dying, the man living off her earnings. Ruby had known a lot of men, she was no innocent, but this man had not taken her for himself. He killed the man for using her, and having her used.

'Is the law chasing you?' he asked Hal Bannion.

Hal answered honestly, because in the short time he'd been face to face with the farmer he figured that he was addressing an honest man, who would see through any lies he told him. 'Yes, sir.'

'Where do you hail from?'

'Crosby Flats.'

'What did you do to have yourself hounded?'

'Nothing.'

'Nothing, huh?' the sod-buster snorted. 'So how come the law is on your tail?'

'It ain't the law doing the chasing. At least not

what you and me would understand the law to be.' Hal wiped his sweat-laden brow. 'I'd be glad to explain, if you'd let me in out of this inferno.'

'Not in the house. The barn.'

'Obliged, mister.'

The shadowed interior of the barn was a true balm to Hal Bannion's sun-tortured body. The farmer followed him in, keeping enough distance between them to knock any thoughts Hal might have about jumping him out of his head.

'I'm listening.'

Hal told him about his troubles that ended with him facing a noose; about Ruth Sullivan's help in busting him out of jail, and his reason for being Mexico bound. After due consideration the farmer accepted his story. Then he gave Bannion some welcome news.

'This preacherman who ain't a preacher, he stopped by here about two weeks ago. His arrival fits in with the start of your troubles.'

'How do you know this Bible-thumper ain't a genuine preacher?' Hal quizzed.

'I know he ain't no preacher, mister, 'cause he had a woman with him he kept pawing, and had an unholy fondness for liquor. In fact, everything a preacher shouldn't be doing, he was doing.'

'Did he say where he was headed?'

'I heard him mention a Mex town, if that's what a shit-hole like San Julio can be rightly called.' He sized Bannion up for a while longer, before he invited, 'Let's go inside the house. Ben Hadley's the name.'

'Howdy, Ben. Hal Bannion's my monicker.' He shook the farmer's hand. 'I'm grateful to you for your hospitality.'

Seated at the table to a meal of cheese, oat bread and water, Hadley aplogized. 'It ain't much, But it'll fill a hole.'

'It's manna from Heaven to me,' Hal assured him.

'When you're finished, you'll find oats in the barn for that mighty fine stallion you're riding.' Hadley studied Bannion for a moment before saying, 'San Julio is a vipers' nest. Are you planning on going there solo?'

'Don't see that there's any other way,' Hal said.

'I can spare a day or two. I know a short cut through the mountains, and I can shoot straight.'

Hal was dumbfounded by the man's generous offer.

'I'd sure like the company, but there could be grief that I wouldn't want to visit on you, Ben.'

'A spell away from this hell-hole will do me good.' He stood up. 'I've got chores to do, and you need rest. We'll leave when the sun loses its spite.'

Jess Bascombe picked at the remains of a thick steak that Ashby had put in the bounty hunter's belly, and opined, 'You know, Ashby' – the saloon owner grimaced at the familiarity, he was used to being addressed as Mr Ashby – 'this feller Bannion didn't look like no killer to me.'

'He's a low-down murderer, that's what Hal Bannion is,' Ashby grated. 'He gunned down a fine upstanding man in Sheriff Bradley. He told him only the night before that he wouldn't stand for the sheriff siding with me in this dispute between me and Bannion.'

Bascombe smiled, showing uneven tobacco-stained teeth. 'Are you that anxious to make this Bannion feller ropebait as a good citizen, or. . . ?' He left the unfinished sentence hang in the air, but there was no mistaking how it should have ended.

Ashby fumed at the bounty-hunter's audacity.

'It don't matter none to me either way. I just get curious when a man wants to spend a thousand of his own dollars.'

He reached over and took a cigar from Ashby's top pocket and lit up, drawing deeply on the rich Cuban tobacco, savouring its smoke as it wafted round him. He blew smoke rings for a spell, letting the saloon owner pick his own time to get off whatever it was that he had on his chest. When he said it, he need not have bothered, because Jess Bascombe knew what he was going to say. He was used to dealing with toads like Ashby, and could read their thoughts and know their words before they uttered them.

'There's, ah. . . . Well, no need to. . . .' He coughed.

'Haul him all the way back to that dangling rope?' Bascombe suggested.

Charles Ashby swallowed hard. He was used to dealing with boot-lickers and idiots; Bascombe was neither. He was a shrewd man, whose eyes bore into Ashby's head and sifted through his thoughts. When the bounty hunter spoke, his barely whispered words were as loud as thunder in the saloon-owner's ears. Ashby glanced anxiously and guiltily around the hotel dining-room, fearing every diner in the room must have heard.

'Murder costs more, Ashby.'

The Cat's Paw owner was about to protest, but saw no point in it; there was no fooling Jess Bascombe.

'How much more?'

'Five thousand dollars.'

Ashby gulped. 'Five thous— You're insane.'

'Of course, that includes keeping our little secret a secret,' Bascombe smiled.

Ashby knew he was over a barrel. He had shown his hand, and had no choice but to accept Bascombe's deal. 'Five thousand it is,' he said resignedly.

'Now.'

'Now?' Ashby gave a constricted shriek.

'Now,' the bounty hunter confirmed.

'You could just ride out of here and keep riding,' Ashby challenged.

'I could.' Bascombe stood up from the table. 'I'll be riding on in a half hour, Ashby. You've got until then to make up your mind.'

He strolled off, then paused and turned. 'Nice beef you've got 'round here.'

Frantically, Alice came downstairs. Luther Bramwell hurried from his office.

'It's Ruth, Pa. I think she's dead.'

FOURTEEN

Hal Bannion came up short, Midnight protesting at the suddeness of its rider's command. Ben Hadley glanced back curiously, his keen grey eyes searching the countryside and the hilly trail ahead for any signs of trouble. There had been some Indian trouble in recent weeks with a handful of bucks who'd left the reservation, and one of Hadley's neighbours had had his throat cut, but there was no proof that Indians had done that foul deed. Being so close to the Mex border, there were a lot of desperate and evil men around, meaner than any Indian.

'What is it, Hal?'

'Just a cold shiver, Ben,' Hal said soulfully.

'In this damn heat?'

Hal Bannion knew in his heart that Ruth Sullivan had died.

'Best not to hang about in these hills,' Hadley

urged, and led off up the twisting trail.

Two hours later, they crossed the Rio Grande to cover the last miles to San Julio.

In Crosby Flats, Charles Ashby was watching a trio of men riding out, trailing spare horses. By rotating the animals, they'd always be on a fresh mount to quickly eat up the miles that Hal Bannion had put between them. Jess Bascombe didn't like the idea of having Speck Spencer and Skeet Blayney along as chaperons.

'I always work alone,' he'd told Ashby.

But the saloon owner had stuck to his guns on having Spencer and Blayney along and, Bascombe, for a thousand more, had agreed.

'When he kills Bannion,' the Cat's Paw owner instructed Spencer and Blayney, 'you plug him, and bring back my damn dollars.'

Bannion and Hadley stopped for grub in an unexpected green oasis in the boiling Mexican terrain, as dusk crept in from the edges of the evening.

'We could make a couple more miles,' Hadley said, 'but I reckon it would be best to camp here for the night. If we leave at first light we should reach San Julio at its sleepiest time of day. That'll give us a chance to reconnoitre.'

'Makes good sense to me,' Hal agreed.

'Bacon, beans and coffee OK?' Hadley enquired.

Bannion nodded his head in agreement and

watched the farmer fetch the makings of the meal from his saddle-bag. He asked the question which had been in his head since Hadley had volunteered to join him, in business that was none of his.

'Why're you doing this, Ben?'

Hadley sat on his haunches slicing bacon. 'Don't know if I have an answer to that. 'Cept maybe being a lawman before being a sod-buster, I've still got it in my blood.'

'Ben Hadley?' Hal's brow creased in thought. 'US Marshal Hadley?'

'That's me.' He waved the frying pan in Hal's face. 'You can't cook bacon without a fire, Hal. Dry wood. Smoke brings the curious.'

Bannion went off to collect an armful of twigs and sticks.

An hour later, bellies full, they lay back and talked, each man giving his life story to the other.

'I met Ruby in Dallas, singing in a saloon,' Hadley told Bannion. 'She was beautiful, with a voice like a nightingale. At first I didn't realize she had upstairs talents as well as a gift for warbling, and by the time I found out I was so smitten I didn't care, figuring that being a married woman would settle her down. . . .' He snorted. 'Well, damn, a lot of men married saloon doves. There weren't that many women to go around. In most cases the woman was glad to leave her old life and embrace the new, and became fine women and good and loving wives. . . .'

As he continued, Ben Hadley's grey eyes became dark pools of sorrow.

'Ruby wasn't one of those women, Hal. Some doves get a liking for saloon shenanigans. Got in Ruby's blood. Or maybe it was always there.' He sighed a thousand year old sigh. 'We tried town living for a spell. I got a job clerking for a freight company, figuring that with me away for long spells Ruby felt lonely and abandoned. I was ready to grasp at any reason to excuse Ruby's sluttish behaviour. I handed in my badge, figuring that if I was around she'd drop her alleycat ways, but she didn't. So, in a final throw of the dice, I became a sod-buster, like my father before me. It didn't make any difference: Ruby only came to life when there were men around; the kind of men that made Ruby glow with excitement. I was a lousy farmer. In the first couple of months I knew that I was a lawman first and a sod-buster a long way behind. It was only a matter of time before Ruby would take off with one of the men who made her glow.'

Hadley went on to tell Hal about killing the man his wife had shacked up with.

'You had just cause, I'd say,' Bannion opined.

'Mebbe, but I was a lawman, Hal. Sworn to uphold the law.'

'You weren't a lawman then.'

'I took an oath,' he said, unforgiving of himself. 'In my reckoning that oath was for life, and I had no right to shunt it aside to vent my spleen.'

He went on to tell Hal of the long months that he'd nursed Ruby, as her body rotted from disease. It was a sad note to end the night on, and Hadley's story brought home to Bannion how fortunate his life had been. Sure he'd had his grief and woe, but his troubles were nothing compared to Ben Hadley's.

Drifting into sleep, Hal vowed that, when he'd cleared his name, he'd go straight to Alice Bramwell and ask her to marry him.

FIFTEEN

The remainder of the trip to San Julio was uneventful, except for a skirmish with a couple of drunks on the town's outskirts that was solved by quick fists and quicker boots. The town was waking, but just. Men with furred up tongues from the revels of the night before were headed to the *cantina* to cure poison with poison. Whereas more *hombres* had never left the *cantina*.

'I figure the watering-hole might be a good starting point to run the reverend to ground,' Hadley opined.

'I guess,' Hal agreed.

'As they hitched their horses to the rail outside the *cantina*, Hadley enquired, 'Has Goodwood ever seen your dial, Hal?'

'No.'

'Then I suggest you do the asking, while I do the watching. I figure that a lot of *hombres* round here might put a name to my face.'

Hal stood at the *cantina* door for a spell, looking in. Entering suddenly from the sun-filled morning would rob him of sight for vital seconds until his eyes became accustomed to the watering-hole's dark interior. When his eyes adjusted, he strolled in and casually made his way to the bar, eyes shifting every which way to the handful of customers in different parts of the *cantina*.

'What weel it be, *señor?*' the paunchy, sweating barkeep asked.

'Beer.'

A moment later, the barkeep placed a warm beer in front of Hal, took payment for the drink, and returned to polishing glasses with a filthy barcloth. Hal could feel the burn of eyes on his back, but resisted the urge to turn around. The questions would come. He was a stranger; an Americano in a Mex town. He could be the law? Also, he could be the hunter or enemy that most of the men in a town like San Julio always expected.

The question came.

'Passing through, stranger?'

Hal turned slowly from the bar, and leaned against it to study the rangy questioner seated with two other men, one definitely a brother, at a table in the furthest and darkest corner of the place.

'I ain't sure of my plans, mister. Should they concern you?'

Hal saw his quizzer stay his brother's hand under the table as he went for iron.

'A mite unfriendly, ain't you?' the man growled.

Hal made a show of relaxing. 'You're right, fella. You'll pardon my bad manners?'

The man nodded his acceptance of Hal's apology. 'I guess no man likes a nose-poker, at that.'

'Will you gents join me?' Bannion invited.

'That's mighty neighbourly,' the man said.

The trio joined Hal at the bar. He ordered the barkeep in friendly banter, 'Dump this cat's piss. Whiskey, and leave the bottle.'

Supping, Hal's questioner introduced himself and his cohorts. 'The name's Jack Spansel.' He ushered forward the man Hal had guessed correctly to be his brother. 'My brother Benny.' The third man, and Hal reckoned the meanest, he introduced as, 'Spotty Beaufort'. He explained, ' 'Cause of all them freckles.'

Hal nodded at each man in turn. 'John Waters,' he lied, not wanting to alert Goodwood if he was still in San Julio by using his real name. He'd be unlikely to forget the name of the man he'd helped Charles Ashby cheat.

'So,' Jack Spansel said, loping an arm around Hal's shoulder, 'now that we're all pals, I reckon we ain't got no secrets from one another. Right, fellas?'

Benny Spansel and Beaufort took to back slapping Hal, Beaufort agreeing. 'No secrets. We've just robbed a bank a spit the other side of the Rio, John.'

'Thought you might be a lawman, come looking,' Benny Spansel added.

'That's the trouble with being self-employed,' Jack Spansel whined: 'The law's got no 'preciation of initiative.' His smile was saintly. 'What's your line of work, John?'

'I'm a rancher. I've come to collect a herd. Mex cows are cheaper.'

'You mean that you're goin' to mix Mex maggot-feeders with good American steers?' Beaufort wailed.

'I'd say that was unpatriotic, John,' Benny Spansel giggled.

Hal stiffened at the change in mood. 'Beef is beef, gents.'

'Did you hear that?' Jack Spansel called out to the other patrons, all of whom were American. 'John here says that Mex cows are as good as American beeves.'

The other men present, recognizing the Spansels and Beaufort's prodding for trouble, began to drift out of the range of any gunplay that might ensue. One of the men that Jack Spansel had addressed acted as the group spokesman.

'Any man says so should be prepared to back his words, I say.'

This brought a chorus of approval from the others.

Hal said. 'I'm not looking for trouble.'

'Ya know what, Brother?' Benny Spansel crooned, pushing close to Hal to sniff at him. 'I think I can smell me a lawman.'

Jack Spansel at first dismissed his brother's assertion.

'Your nose ain't ever been right since that mule flattened it last year, Benny.' Now Jack Spansel made a big deal of sniffing Hal, even going on his knees, much to everyone's amusement, to sniff Hal's boots. He stood up, his smile fading in direct ratio to his changing stance. 'Ya know, John Waters, if that's your damn name, my brother's called it right, I reckon.'

'No, he ain't,' Hal said. 'I'm a rancher, like I said.'

Jack Spansel growled, 'And I say you're a liar, mister.'

Hal swiped the whiskey bottle he held across Jack Spansel's skull, and hoped that Ben Hadley was ready to back his play, because if he wasn't, Bannion knew as sure as night followed day that San Julio would be his graveyard.

Jack Spansel staggered backwards, his hand going to the jagged scalp wound that the broken whiskey bottle had opened up. Blood streamed down his forehead into his eyes. Surprise handed Hal the advantage, which he grabbed. His right boot flashed, and Spotty Beaufort doubled over whimpering like a dying animal, nursing his groin. Hal caught sight of Benny Spansel's Colt flashing from its holster to his mitt with eye-blinding speed.

Where the hell was Ben Hadley?

SIXTEEN

'Freeze!' Benny Spansel ordered.

Bannion's side-swipe paused in mid air under the threat of the hardcase's cocked gun.

'I could have killed him, Jack,' he boasted, 'but I reckoned you'd want to mutilate this bastard personally.'

'You got that right, Brother,' Jack Spansel glowered, landing a pile-driver in Hal's belly that sent the *cantina* into a spin.

'How d'ya wanna do it?' Beaufort asked Jack Spansel, as he gripped Hal in a bone-crunching armlock.

Jack Spansel thought for a moment, then his eyes glowed evilly. 'Haul him outside.'

Hal fought every step of the way, but there were plenty of willing hands to help the Spansels and Beaufort. As they tied him to the back of a wagon commandeered at gunpoint from a passer-by, the question uppermost in Hal Bannion's mind was, where the hell had Ben Hadley got to?

If he had looked to the roof of the *cantina*, his question would have been answered. Hadley was there, Winchester primed.

'Hold it right there,' he ordered the Spansels. He included Spotty Beaufort, as his hand slid to his gun. 'You, too.' And backed his threat when Beaufort crouched to send lead his way. Hadley's single bullet took off the crown of Beaufort's head. The wagon horse, already edgy, was spooked by the crack of Hadley's rifle and reared wildly. Its kicking feet shattered a support beam of the *cantina* overhang, bringing the flimsy structure crashing down on the men exiting the saloon, intent on seeing Hal turned to raw meat on the stony street.

Two men dived from under the collapsing overhang, just as the Spansel brothers leaped in the opposite direction, giving them the chance to catch Hadley in a crossfire, their guns already free of leather.

Bannion pulled his hands free of the loosely tied rope that Hadley's intervention had robbed Jack Spansel of time to tighten, his pistol flashed and one of the duo who had thrown in with the Spansels, a red-haired gent, fell, and rolled on the ground trying to keep in his spilling guts. Hadley's rifle spat, and Benny Spansel's face collapsed, a split-second before the back of his head exploded. Jack Spansel winged Hadley, spinning him about and tumbling him off the *cantina* roof, to lie winded on the hard ground. Hal turned his gun on Jack Spansel, shattering his kneecap and, as his leg buckled under him, Bannion put a second slug plumb centre of his chest. Frothy blood spilled through Jack Spansel's grimacing lips, his eyes rolled and he crashed on to his back with a vacant stare.

The remaining man stood in terrified silence. 'Please, mister,' he pleaded with Hal, 'I just got sucked into this.'

Bannion let him sweat before he said, 'Get out of my sight.'

The man vaulted into leather and galloped down the street, glancing back every couple of seconds to make sure his luck was holding. Bannion went to help Hadley up, evoking a howl from the pain of his busted left shoulder.

'Is there a doc in this hangdog town?' Hal enquired of the gathering crowd.

'A horse doctor, meester,' a Mexican boy told him.

'If that's all you've got, lead the way,' Hal said, tossing the youngster a dollar from Hadley's pocket, that lit the boy's eyes like harvest moons.

'I ain't going to be much good to you, if you have to haul that shyster preacher back to Crosby Flats,' Hadley said.

'You've done more than enough already,' Hal

replied, 'and I'm beholden to you, Ben.'

Hadley laughed. 'You know, I enjoyed that little shindig.'

Bannion left Hadley in the vet's care and went in search of the Reverend Goodwood.

Jess Bascombe filled his canteen from the water-hole and tasted the water. 'Tastes like rat's piss,' was the verdict. He emptied the canteen over his head and then refilled it. 'Are you boys thirsty?' he enquired of Spencer and Blayney, who had kept their distance from Bascombe all the way from Crosby Flats. The Ashby duo had been unnerved a couple of times on seeing Indians. 'There ain't nothin' to worry about,' Bascombe had assured them. 'If an Indian wants to kill you, you won't see him until he's good and ready.'

Spencer was first from the saddle and Blayney followed his lead seconds after. Bascombe stood back from the water-hole to let them drink. They both froze when they heard the click of the bounty-hunter's gun hammer.

'Now, tell me, exactly when were you boys thinkin' of back-shootin' good old Jess Bascombe?'

'Back-shoot ya?' Spencer chuckled nervously. 'That's a loco idea.'

'I'll ask the question again' – there was ice in Bascombe's tone – 'and if you lie to me, again, I'll drop you both where you stand. Understood?'

Skeet Blayney swung around uninvited and

Bascombe's bullet spat dirt in his face, a stone gouging a furrow along his right cheek from his nose to his ear. 'Don't move so fast,' Bascombe rebuked. 'It's dangerous.'

Unnerved, Blayney gabbled, 'Ashby said when you'd killed Bannion, we was to plug you.'

Speck Spencer glared contemptuously at his partner, but he was glad Blayney had lost his nerve first, because another second and he'd have spilled the beans about Ashby's plan himself.

Blayney whined pleadingly, 'Spencer and me can ride outa here right now, Mr Bascombe.'

Stonily, Bascombe declared, 'From now on you fellas ride in front of me.'

'Are you goin' to kill us?' Blayney asked.

'Maybe. Then again, maybe not. I ain't made up my mind yet.'

Hal Bannion stepped through the bead curtains of Madame Rosa's, the fanciest house in San Julio, proving that pandering to a man's libido paid handsomely. Two of the rouged ladies stretched out on plush settees came to link Hal on either side. The younger of the two in years, but the older in know-how, Hal reckoned, purred. 'I am Lolo. I show you a good time, Americano, eh?'

'He is mine, beetch,' the other whore spat. Turning to Hal, she introduced herself, 'I am Rosita, *señor*. I know a lot of tricks.'

Hal smiled. 'I guess you do, Rosita, and you're

real pretty Lolo, but I'm here to see Madame Rosa herself.'

'She no bed men,' Lolo groused. 'She, boss.'

'Did I hear my name?'

Hal swung around to see a mountain of a woman, all-American and black, standing in the open doorway of a very plush sitting-room.

'You're Madame Rosa?' Hal enquired.

'And who would you be?'

'The name's John Waters,' Hal lied again.

'Hello John,' Rosa chuckled, her voice deeper than any man's. 'State your business.'

'I'm looking for a man—'

Rosa chuckled. 'If I might be so bold as to say so, John, your preference isn't obvious in your gait.'

Hal blushed sunset red. 'I ain't looking for a man to . . . well, to. . . .'

The cathouse madam's amusement heightened. 'I know what you mean, John. What man would you he looking for?'

'A preacher. Only he ain't a preacher. . . .'

Rosa put a hand to her forehead. 'I do declare that you have my head reeling, John.'

'Goes by the name of Goodwood.'

'A preacher, in a house of the flesh, John?'

'Like I said, this fella wears spots he's got no call to show. He likes cards, whiskey and women.'

'My kind of preacher,' Rosa purred. She strolled to where Hal stood, every ounce of her enormous poundage wobbling. 'If I knew of such a preacher, why would you want to see him, John?'

'He helped cheat my brother out of our ranch, and then as good as pulled the trigger that killed him,' Bannion said grimly.

Rosa considered Hal for a lingering moment before she replied, 'Goodwood, huh? Well, John Waters, I don't know of any Reverend Goodwood.'

Bannion sighed despondently. 'I thank you anyway.'

He was at the front door when Rosa said, 'But I do know of a Reverend Peabody.'

'Peabody?'

'Likes poker, whiskey and women.'

Hal felt a thrill of excitement race through him. 'Where would I find this Reverend Peabody?'

'About three miles south of town. Shacked up with a *cantina* whore who's probably given him six different kinds of pox by now.'

Hal kissed the black woman enthusiastically on both cheeks. 'Obliged, Rosa.'

'Stop that this instant, John Waters,' she chided playfully. 'My, you could turn a girl's head something awful.'

Anxiously Hal enquired, 'Three miles south of town, you say?'

'Yeah. About two miles out you'll come to a fork in the road. Take the left trail. You'll come to a creek. Above the creek there's a stand of spindly timber. It's there you'll find Peabody or Goodwood's shack.'

Hal thanked Rosa again, and quickly sought the door.

'You be careful, John,' she warned. 'The reverend's trickier and meaner than a cornered rattler.'

'I'll be careful,' Bannion assured her.

'If you want I could pleasure you myself, John Waters,' she invited, 'When you've finished your business with the Reverend Peabody.'

'That's a real good offer, Rosa,' Hal complimented, and meant it. 'The thing is, I've got me a real fine woman waiting for me whom I'm anxious to get back to.'

'Good luck, John Waters,' Rosa sighed wistfully.

Hal hit the street and lost no time in heading south.

SEVENTEEN

Jess Bascombe looked down on San Julio from the rocky pass that overlooked the settlement, and at the rider beating a fast trail out of town. 'Some fella's sure in a real hurry to leave,' he mumbled.

'That's Hal Bannion,' Spencer confirmed.

'We could cut him off if we hurry,' Skeet Blayney contributed.

'We ain't in no hurry,' Bascombe drawled.

'Bannion could slip the loop,' Spencer warned.

'He's a man in a hurry, I reckon on an errand.' Bascombe leisurely regained his saddle. 'I figure he's found this preacherman your boss is so worried he'll find. He'll haul him back to town and rest up before he makes the return trip to Crosby Flats.'

Spencer panicked. 'He'll mouth with Goodwood and learn 'bout Ashby cheatin' his brother out of their ranch.'

'Won't matter none,' Bascombe said. setting off at an easy canter, 'dead men can't talk.'

*

Hal burned trail like a madman until he reached the fork in the road which Rosa had described. He chose the left junction as the cathouse madam had instructed him to, and ten minutes later he reached the creek.

He looked to the rise of ground above the creek topped by spindly trees, and the narrow twisting trail leading to it through boulders that would provide an ambusher with perfect cover. The trail ran over hard ground. He scanned the other option, a trail with little or no cover, but with shale underfoot. The track would be impossible to negotiate without loose shale rattling down into the creek, and that could alert Goodwood to any callers.

The reverend had chosen well. Any uninvited visitor was left with two choices, both of which were unhealthy. Hal could not see the shack, but that did not mean that the shack-dweller could not see him.

He chose the boulder trail.

Leaving the horse doctor's office, his shoulder set as good as Pedro Martinez could set it, Ben Hadley quickly stepped into the alley nearby, his interest fully on the three riders drawing rein outside the *cantina*. The tallest he knew; the others he did not, but if they were riding with Jess Bascombe they were men decent folk would shun.

Hadley had crossed trails a time or two with

the bounty hunter/cum gun-for-hire, and reckoned that he was the kind of parasite that poisoned the West, and made it the dangerous land it was. He pulled back into the alley as Bascombe appeared to glance casually along the town's main street, but Hadley knew there was nothing casual about the manhunter's perusal. In the brief glance, Bascombe had seen every speck of dust.

The trio went inside the *cantina*. Hadley wondered where Hal Bannion had got to. Goodwood's seeker had proved to be handy with a gun, but running into Jess Bascombe, if he was looking for Bannion, and Hadley would bet that the bounty hunter's visit to San Julio was not coincidental, would be asking too much of the rancher's prowess.

Hadley thought hard. Where would Hal Bannion have begun his search for the phoney reverend? He got his answer as he saw Madam Rosa sipping tea on the cathouse balcony.

Bannion's progress was slow, and his heart thumped with the expectancy of feeling the thump of a bullet in his body any second. He was regretting his hasty departure from town; he should have waited until Ben Hadley was able to accompany him. Even busted up the way he was, Hal reckoned that the ex-US marshal would still be an asset. He cursed his hot-headed eagerness in lighting out the way he had.

He resisted the urge to approach the shack, gun-ready, figuring that his plan of arriving under the guise of an innocent traveller might serve him best. It was a gamble that could send him winging to his Maker, if Goodwood decided to shoot first and ask questions later.

His luck holding, Hal came out of the trees to see a middle-aged, much used Mexican woman washing clothes in a wooden tub, apparently unaware of his arrival.

'Ma'am. . . .'

The woman turned slowly, and that was what alerted Hal. It told him that she was expecting him and her washing was play-acting, designed to put the caller at his ease. In the kind of danger-laden terrain that the border territory was, with its constant threat of mayhem, the woman would have spun around at his hailing of her. She would not have turned slowly.

Grabbing his Winchester Hal flung himself from the saddle just as a pistol flashed from the side of the shack. The bullet buzzed off the saddle horn and whined away to die. Bannion rolled down a knoll into the cover of the weakling trees, his rifle spitting twice in the general direction of the shack. The woman screamed and scampered indoors. Hal, on reaching cover, quickly sought a better sighting of the bushwhacker, but the shooter had also changed location and was now hiding behind a stack of firewood on which Bannion's bullets would make little impact.

Hal could crouch in the trees all day, and Goodwood could hide behind the woodpile all day too, with the open ground between them holding certain death for the man who entered its domain.

It was a stand-off.

EIGHTEEN

'Wha'd'ya want, stranger?' Goodwood called out.

'Is your handle Goodwood?' Hal hailed back.

'What if it is?' back came the griping reply.

'Name's Bannion.'

'I know lotsa names, mister. Why should I remember yours?'

'The shake in your voice says you do,' Hal growled. 'You and me've got business back in Croshy Flats with Charles Ashby, Reverend.'

The so-called preacher cut loose with wild, panicky gunfire. Hal's accurate return fire peppered the woodpile, spinning logs into the air.

'What you've got to decide now, Reverend, is, do you want to die for Charles Ashby? Because die you will, if you don't see sense!' Hal shouted.

Hal spun round at the crack of a twig behind him and his trigger was three quarter ways pulled before he recognized Ben Hadley.

'That was a fool thing to do!' he berated the ex-lawman.

'What did you expect me to do,' Hadley returned crankily, 'make an official announcement of my arrival?'

Hal Bannion's scowl turned to a smile. 'Glad to see you, Ben. Maybe you'd have an idea or two as to how this stand-off can be resolved.'

'I reckon I might have, Hal Bannion.' His return smile was the kind that marked a new, yet old friendship.

A minute later, Ben Hadley was laying heavy fire on the woodpile to keep Goodwood at bay, while Hal Bannion climbed a tree with the agility of a monkey. When he reached its top branches, he had a clear view of Goodwood's position behind the woodpile.

The shyster preacher readily recognized Hadley's strategy, but was left with no choice but to remain where he was, prevented from fleeing by Hadley's hail of lead. Now, as Hadley paused to reload, he grabbed his chance to dive for the rear of the shack, from which he'd be safe even from Hal's high vantage point.

Bannion opened up to pepper the ground round Goodwood as he broke from the cover of the wood-pile, sending him into a leaping jig as bullets bit at his boots. Hal swore as he gained new cover, but could do nothing about it. Goodwood dead, was no good at all.

'Give it up, Goodwood,' Hal hollered. 'The next time I'll stop your pump.'

The Reverend Goodwood quickly assessed his options. Two against one was not a healthy situation to be in, with both men gun-handier than he was. It didn't take long for him to reach a decision. He threw his pistol into the clearing in front of the shack. 'If you fellas just said you was calling, there'd have been no need for all this lead slinging,' he laughed. 'I'm coming out. You ask whatever you want, mister,' he called to Bannion, 'about Ashby's shenanigans.'

A minute later, under threat of Bannion and Hadley's guns, Goodwood's tongue was loosened and Hal learned all about Charles Ashby's scheme to cheat John Bannion and get his hands on the Broken Spur.

'I should kill you like I would a wild dog!' Hal told Goodwood.

Ben Hadley pulled Bannion back as the preacher thumped to the ground under Bannion's double-fisted assault.

On the outskirts of San Julio, Bannion and Hadley came up with their next plan for survival. Hal would head into town on his own with Goodwood in tow to draw Bascombe's attention, while. . . .

'I'll make my way through the backlots,' Hadley explained.

Plan of action agreed, Hal rode on up the town's main street. Speck Spencer, sitting outside the *cantina*, scampered back inside. A second later, the bounty hunter and Skeet Blayney put in an appearance, flanked by Spencer.

'A bit out of your neck of the woods, ain't you?' Hal said, addressing Spencer and Blayney. The Ashby duo's eyes were on Goodwood, while Jess Bascombe's attention was exclusively on Hal. 'Doing Ashby's dirty work, fellas?' This time Hal included Bascombe in his remarks.

'Have you spilled your guts?' Spencer asked the sweating Goodwood.

'I know everything,' Hal confirmed. 'And as soon as I get back to Crosby Flats, Ashby will be all washed up. If I were you, fellas, I'd stay south of the border.'

Bannion rode on, as Blayney taunted, 'It won't matter any, Bannion.'

Bascombe stepped into the street. 'Ashby's paid me to kill you, Bannion,' he stated flatly. 'I aim to earn his dollars.'

'Hello, Bascombe.'

The bounty hunter froze, and his eyes slid to where Ben Hadley was emerging from an alley, his rifle directed at him.

'Well, now, if it isn't Ben Hadley, boys,' Bascombe exclaimed to Spencer and Blayney.

'Who the hell is Ben Hadley?' Spencer wanted to know.

The manhunter explained. 'Mr Hadley used to be a U.S. marshal' – his smile changed to a sneer, 'before he married a saloon whore, who remained a whore.'

'Don't do it, Ben,' Bannion pleaded, as Hadley's temper flared. 'He ain't worth wasting a bullet on.'

Bascombe removed his hat and scratched his head. 'Do you think I could take you, Hadley?'

Hadley slung his rifle to Hal. 'If you want that question answered, now's the time, Bascombe.'

'You see,' Hadley explained to Spencer and Blayney, 'that's a question that's been hangin' round for a long time fellas.' Then he turned back to Hadley. 'And you know what? I reckon that today is not the day to have it answered.'

Jess Bascombe strode off to his horse.

'You're running out?' Spencer flared.

'Yep,' the bounty hunter answered simply.

'You yellow bastard!' Blayney swore.

It was his last oath. It died on his lips as Jess Bascombe's gun spat.

'Ashby ain't goin' to like this,' Speck Spencer threatened.

'I reckon I don't have to worry none about Ashby, Spencer,' Bascombe laughed. 'Like Mr Bannion said, Ashby's all washed up.'

Spencer stood alone.

'I should kill you, Spencer,' Hal growled.

'He ain't worth a bullet either, Hal,' Hadley said.

'I guess he's not at that,' Bannion agreed.

NINETEEN

On hearing the commotion on Main, Charles Ashby hurried eagerly to the saloon door. What he saw was what he'd never expected to see. Sweat broke instantly on his brow when he saw Hal Bannion riding in with Goodwood in tow, accompanied by another man who had lawman written all over him.

The trio were headed straight for the Cat's Paw.

Ashby scurried back through the saloon to the rear office, where he dived for the safe and grabbed what he could, stuffing his pockets with its contents. He looked longingly at what he had to leave behind, but concluded sensibly, 'Better half rich than whole dead.'

He raced for the saloon's rear exit, to stop dead in his tracks on coming face to face with Hal Bannion at the other side of the door.

'Look what I found, Ben,' he said. 'A rat leaving

his sinking ship.' Hal shoved Ashby back all the way to his office, and then demanded, 'I'll have what you stole from my brother, Ashby, and be quick in handing it over, because I'm working hard not to kill you where you stand.'

Ashby spilled his pockets on to the desk, and then added the remaining contents of the safe. 'It's all yours if you want, Hal. I'd say a fair price for a horse out of town, wouldn't you?'

Hal sifted through the papers until he found what he wanted, the deeds of the Broken Spur and John Bannion's markers. 'I've got all I want, Ashby. You're going to swing for murder.'

Hal grabbed a whining Ashby and hauled him off to jail. Slamming the cell door shut on the saloon owner, Hal speculated, 'You know, Ben. This town is going to need a good, honest lawman from now on, and the job's vacant.'

Ben Hadley smiled. 'You know, Hal. I think I've had my bellyful of sod-busting, at that.'

Hal Bannion placed the bunch of wild flowers on Ruth Sullivan's grave, which was right alongside John Bannion's. He took Alice Bramwell's hand in his and strolled off across the meadow, through the fine Mexican horses that were feeding contentedly on the rich grass, almost ready now to be sold to the army.

'I guess it's time to go and talk to your pa, Alice,' he said.

'I reckon so, Hal Bannion,' Alice replied, hugging close to him.

'Do you think he'll welcome a Bannion into the family?'

'Don't much care,' Alice said. 'Here's one Bramwell who'll be more than proud to be a Bannion.'

Hal sat on the stump of a tree on a hill overlooking the meadow, his arm around Alice. After the honeymoon he'd have a journey to make, back to Mexico, back to Miguel Santos.

Then, all his accounts would be settled.